"Actually, I came over to ask you to marry me."

Lauren was completely and totally nonplussed.

"The fact is, I'm not asking you, I'm begging you. Just for the next few days or so." He watched her closely, trying to gauge her reaction. When there was none, he forged ahead. "I don't know what else to do. When Granny woke up from her nap, she wanted to know where you were.... If we don't play along with her little fantasy, anything could happen."

Lauren was still reeling. Not helping David seemed unnecessarily cruel. On the other hand, becoming entangled in his problem was something she did *not* relish. But she couldn't hurt a sweet old lady, just because she was fed up with the male population....

Dear Reader,

Celebration 1000! continues in May with more wonderful books by authors you've loved for years and so many of your new favorites!

Starting with . . . *The Best Is Yet To Be* by Tracy Sinclair. Bride-to-be Valentina Richardson finally meets Mr. Right. Too bad he's her fiancé's best friend!

Favorite author Marie Ferrarella brings us BABY'S CHOICE—an exciting new series where matchmaking babies bring their unsuspecting parents together!

The FABULOUS FATHERS continue with Derek Wolfe, a *Miracle Dad.* A fanciful and fun-filled romance from Toni Collins.

This month we're very pleased to present our *debut* author, Carolyn Zane, with her first book, *The Wife Next Door.* In this charming, madcap romance, neighbors David Barclay and Lauren Wills find that make-believe marriage can lead to the real thing!

Carol Grace brings us a romantic contest of wills in the *The Lady Wore Spurs.* And don't miss *Race to the Altar* by Patricia Thayer.

In June and July, look for more exciting Celebration 1000! books by Debbie Macomber, Elizabeth August, Annette Broadrick and Laurie Paige. We've planned this event for you, our wonderful readers. So, stake out your favorite easy chair and get ready to fall in love all over again with Silhouette Romance.

Happy reading!

Anne Canadeo
Senior Editor
Silhouette Romance

Please address questions and book requests to:
Reader Service
U.S.: P.O. Box 1325, Buffalo, NY 14269
Canadian: P.O. Box 1050, Niagara Falls, Ont. L2E 7G7

THE WIFE
NEXT DOOR
Carolyn Zane

Silhouette
R O M A N C E™
Published by Silhouette Books
America's Publisher of Contemporary Romance

To the good Lord, who has blessed me so richly.

THANKS

To my best friend and husband, Matt, for believing in me.
To my family and friends for their encouragement.
Especially, Jeff, Elizabeth, Mom, Dad and Judy.

ACKNOWLEDGMENT

Thank you, Andre, for knowing how to spell.

 SILHOUETTE BOOKS

ISBN 0-373-19011-5

THE WIFE NEXT DOOR

Copyright © 1994 by Carolyn Pizzuti

CAROLYN ZANE

lives with her husband, Matt, and their two cats, Jazz and Blues, in the lush, rolling countryside near Portland, Oregon's Willamette River. When she is not producing local TV commercials, or helping her husband renovate their rambling one-hundred-and-twenty-three-year-old farmhouse, she works out, travels with friends, makes her own clothes and finds time, here and there, to write.

A Note from the Author

Dear Reader,

As a fan of romantic comedy and theatrical farce, it's my feeling that falling in love can be a very funny proposition. In my mind, the sexiest man is a man with a sense of humor. A man who can roll with the punches when things get crazy. A man who has the ability to make others laugh and the self-confidence to laugh at himself. Hence, the hero for *The Wife Next Door* was born.

It is my extreme pleasure to be included as part of Celebration 1000! This being my first effort for Silhouette, it is indeed a time to celebrate. To be published among some of Silhouette's finest authors at this milestone is truly an honor.

I feel very fortunate for two reasons: to be a part of Celebration 1000!, and to have a husband who not only laughs at himself, but who laughs with me.

Best wishes always,

Carolyn Zane

Chapter One

Pike Street Market Place in Seattle was bustling with the first Christmas shoppers of the year. The open-air market on Elliott Bay was a colorful riot of confusion as the mad swarm searched for that perfect something for the person who has everything.

Jugglers juggled, singers sang, mimes mimed, and panhandlers panhandled. The fish market was in full swing, all forms of fresh seafood were flying over the heads of a delighted crowd. It was definitely cold enough to snow. The air had that quiet, almost eerie feeling that comes right before the first flakes begin to fall.

Lauren Wills paused to examine a pair of handcrafted silver earrings at one of the dozens of jewelry booths. Heaving the sigh of one whose heart has just been broken, she came to the unfortunate realization that for her, this Christmas was going to be nothing but a series of sad and painful memories. And though she was in the midst of hundreds of smiling people, she'd never felt so alone in her life. Or so angry.

Shuffling along with the throng, she decided that the small Market Place Café was just what she needed. Maybe its warmth and a strong jolt of caffeine would put her in a better frame of mind.

The view from her small corner booth revealed a very foggy Elliott Bay. Soulful sea gull cries echoed Lauren's mood as she shrugged out of her coat and ordered a triple espresso. She wanted to scream, too. Scream at Joe.

Why did he have to choose right now to go through a midlife crisis? "The conceited overgrown Ken doll," she muttered, glancing around sheepishly to see if anyone was watching her talk to herself.

How could he do this to her? Especially now, just a few weeks before the mayor's Christmas ball. She couldn't go to the most prestigious event of the year without a date. How mortifying.

The waitress lumbered over and pushed the espresso at Lauren with a curious look. "You been in here before, honey?"

"No, I don't think so." Lauren arranged her lips into what she hoped resembled a smile.

"Funny, I could swear I know you from somewhere. Have a nice day." She frowned thoughtfully and scratched her head with her pencil as she walked away.

"Thank you," Lauren nodded at her retreating back. She knew the woman had probably seen her on the evening news show she anchored. It happened all the time, and usually Lauren got a kick out of her viewing public, but today she wasn't in the mood. Today she was the anchor who'd been thrown overboard. Film at eleven.

Limply she stirred her espresso as her thoughts drifted to Joe. And Tanya. And Joe taking Tanya to the mayor's Christmas ball. Tossing back a healthy slug of the thick, dark coffee, she remembered the first time she'd seen Joe, three years before.

It had been her twenty-sixth birthday and she'd been covering a story about a local fashion designer for the news program she now anchored. Joe had been modeling the latest in underwear for men. With sun-bleached hair and a tropical tan, he'd been the typical beach boy next door. Such a long time ago it now seemed. Tanya probably hadn't been born yet, Lauren thought sourly.

Finishing her drink, she dropped some money on the table and left the café. The caffeine hadn't helped.

She trudged up the hill to her condo, pausing to catch her breath and pull her colorful scarf up over her chin. The streetlight overhead buzzed on as snowflakes swirled and danced in its beam.

They had presented a striking couple. Lauren, with her tall, dark beauty, had been the perfect complement to Joe. He was an easy guy to date, not too bright, but lovable in a self-absorbed kind of way. He had never pushed for a serious relationship or commitment, and that had been fine with Lauren. She'd been on her way to the anchor desk, and Joe had been on his way to the cover of *GQ*. Joe had been perfect for her life-style.

Okay, so it hadn't been the most passionate of relationships. Oh, the kisses had been pleasant.... No real fireworks, but hey, they'd had fun together. She'd been comfortable with Joe. She'd counted on Joe. Whenever she'd needed a quick date to a social function, for the past three years, she'd just dialed good ol' Joe. Until Tanya. Twenty-two-year-old, exotic looking supermodel Tanya. His soul mate, he'd said.

Lauren crossed her eyes and stuck out her tongue. *Soul mate?*

"Fine, Joe. When you come to your senses, don't come crying to me," Lauren had flung at him, hurt and angry that he wanted to date someone else.

"Don't worry about me, Lauren. Worry about yourself. You're so wrapped up in your job, life is passing you by. You can't live without me. I'm afraid you'll never go out again," Joe had arrogantly informed her.

As Lauren's temper rose, so did the pace of her walk, until she was nearly jogging up the hill to her condo.

"Can't live without you? Ha!" she muttered, her breath coming in short, puffy clouds. "What a jerk!" she spat much to the surprise of a passerby. "Merry Christmas," she said, smiling brightly, and continued on her ill-tempered way.

She could live without him just fine, thank you very much, and she would prove it. What she needed here was revenge, preferably in the form of an extraordinarily handsome date to the mayor's ball. But how? Who? She was out of practice with this sort of thing. Well, she had time. The ball was still several weeks away. Surely by then she'd be able to find a single, willing man, her age, as good-looking as or better than Joe. Too bad she couldn't just skip the whole thing, but the station was making her attendance mandatory. Image, they'd said.

Turning down her street, she began reviewing possibilities in her mind. All the men she worked with were already married or taken. Except, of course, for an eager young intern from the University of Washington. She considered and rejected him. No, they should at least be old enough to shave. Who else did she know? Besides her father and brother, no one. Work had been her life. Work and Joe ... the fink.

"Fink, fink, fink!"

"Pardon me, Miss Wills?" The security guard at the high rise building where she lived looked at her in surprise. Lauren hadn't realized she'd spoken out loud.

"Oh, not you, Gordon. I was, ah ... just trying to ah ... *think*. Think, think, think!"

"Well, keep up the good work, Miss Wills." Gordon beamed.

"Thanks, I ... will," Lauren said as the elevator door closed. That does it. I'm losing it. And all because of that selfish, thoughtless, creep Joe. Pushing the button to her floor, she decided she'd better call Polly. Wasn't that what best friends were for? To find blind dates for people in dire straits? Although, considering Polly was a kindergarten teacher, she might not be much help.

The elevator doors opened, and Lauren marched out and down the hall to her door. "Forget you, Mr. Soul Mate," she mumbled as she set her purse on the floor and crouched down next to it, searching its cavernous depths for her keys. "I'll round up some handsome hunk and you'll be— Oof!" Suddenly, the air was knocked out of Lauren's lungs, and she found herself sprawled unceremoniously in front of her door.

"Oh! Sorry! I didn't see you there!"

Lauren tried to speak, but could only emit small, wheezing gasps. She felt someone kneel down beside her. Concern was evident in his touch.

"Are you okay? I'm really sorry. I wasn't looking where I was going. I heard someone talking, and I should have..." his voice trailed off.

Turning, Lauren looked up into two of the most beautiful green eyes she'd ever seen. Not an ordinary green, really, more of an emerald, with tiny gold sparkles in them. And the thickest black lashes... "No, no, I'm okay. Really." She tried to hide her mortification by smiling as she struggled to sit up. "I, uh, was talking to...uh, practicing...er, for a play. A Western play," she improvised. "About a roundup. My lines...you know." She blushed furiously. *A Western play?* Why was she lying to this Greek god?

"Sounds interesting." He grinned and helped her to her feet. Clearly it was not the play that was interesting to him, as his eyes broke contact with hers to sweep the slender but shapely body her coat could not hide. He held out his hand to her.

"I'm David Barclay, your new neighbor. I just moved in across the hall." He gestured to his front door. "I'm really sorry about knocking you over. I've had a lot on my mind lately, and I guess I didn't see you. I was just on my way out when I heard you...rehearsing." Again the devastating grin.

"Lauren Wills." She took his hand and froze as she felt his warm, strong hand grasp hers in what had to be the sexiest handshake she'd ever experienced. He was just over six feet tall, with wavy black hair and handsome, outdoorsy looks. Wow, if this guy was single and could dance, he was just what the doctor ordered.

"My hand?"

"Oh, sorry!" Lauren jerked her hand away and laughed nervously. "Well, I should go...rehearse." *Rehearse?* If she didn't get inside quick, she was afraid she might blurt out some even more outlandish fib. Why stop at actress? Her behavior was scaring her.

"I know this may sound clichéd, but have we met before?"

"Around the building, maybe?"

"That must be it." He didn't look too sure. "Well, I'd better get going. My grandmother's waiting for me, and visiting hours have already begun at the hospital."

Lauren shifted her purse to her other arm and looked at him with sympathy. "It's nothing serious, I hope?"

"Well, not now. It was touch and go for a while there." A range of emotions danced across his handsome face. It was obvious that he cared a great deal for his grandmother. "She's suffered a mild heart attack."

"Oh, no. That's too bad."

"Yeah. Thank God she's feeling better now. She's a great lady." He stuffed his hands into the pockets of his jacket. "I've been in kind of a daze lately, I'm sure that's why I ran over you just now. She's been on my mind."

"No doubt. Well, I'm glad she's okay...." Lauren finished lamely. She never knew what to say in these situations.

"Thanks. It was nice bumping into you." His eyes twinkled.

Another handshake. The same thrilling, sexy, electric handshake. He tightened his grip slightly and released her hand, and his face registered a momentary look of surprise.

She felt light-headed. If a simple handshake with him could do this to her, what would dancing together be like?

"I guess I'll see you around." He smiled, revealing a deep dimple in his left cheek, and turned to head for the elevator.

Lauren watched him walk away—and what a walk it was. Snug blue jeans surrounded long legs, and the kind of shapely rear end that made football interesting. He was wearing a leather jacket that showed off his broad shoulders, and cowboy boots, of all things. *I'm really something,* she thought as she finally located her keys and let herself into her condo. I break up with my boyfriend of over three years, and less than a day later I'm fantasizing about dancing with the cowboy next door. She sighed and slammed the door.

David Barclay eased his Jeep out of the underground parking garage and into the late-afternoon traffic. Thank heaven for four-wheel drive. The snow was starting to fall in earnest, and he was beginning to wonder if he should attempt the drive up to the small town of Sea Grove, where Gran lived. No matter. She needed him, and he'd be there for her. Just as she'd always been there for him. Abigail Barclay had raised him from the time he was eight years old. His parents had parted in a bitter, messy divorce that left no room in their lives for a hurting little boy. Neither of them had lived very long after the divorce. Gran had always said they'd died of broken hearts, but David knew better. If anything, they'd driven each other to an early grave.

So Gran had stepped in like a trooper. A state trooper, he mused. He hadn't been a bad kid, but, like any growing boy, he could be a handful. Luckily, Gran had been up to the task.

She'd patched and kissed boo-boos, baked a better chocolate chip cookie than Mrs. Fields, and helped build a tree fort in the backyard that rivaled the Swiss Family Robinson's. She'd sewed Boy Scout patches on his uniform, whupped his bottom when he was "uppity," and cussed the ref loud enough at his Little League games to stop play.

David pulled off the freeway and started the long, slippery drive on the winding road out to Sea Grove Community Hospital. If he was a good driver, it was because of Gran. She'd been sixty-five when she taught him to drive.

David turned on the high beams and the snow sliced through the extra light with an angry flurry. *Great night to be out.* He didn't care. He was doing it for Gran. He'd do anything for her. She'd encouraged him to stay in law school, and she'd stayed up late more than one night to help him study for the bar. And when he had passed, no one had been prouder than Gran. Grandma. Rock-solid. Invincible. Until Bert died. Grandpa Bertrand Barclay had been the love of her life. And when he had passed away, part of Gran had seemed to pass away with him.

David pushed the automatic scan button on his car radio, searching for driving conditions. Not that it would help much at this point. Well, it wasn't far now, anyway. He reached over and switched off the radio.

Why Gran insisted on living in that gargantuan relic out in Sea Grove was more than he could understand sometimes. Abigail wasn't the tough old bird she used to be. She had the mind and wit of a woman half her age, but at eighty, her health was beginning to fail. Her heart had been giving her problems for years now, and David worried about her, living so far out.

At least she had Rose. Rose Chesterton was Abigail's nurse, chauffeur, cook, companion and bodyguard. Good-natured Rose. If anyone could take care of and protect Gran, it was Rose. She was almost as wide as she was tall, and she was tall. Very tall. Taller than David, and he was six-foot-one. Abigail said she loved having Rose live with her since Bert's death, because if the house ever caught fire, Rose could save her *and* all the furniture. David didn't know about that. Rose got winded bowling.

And there was Abigail's neighbor, Dr. Homer Penwalt. Seventy-something, and still rode his bicycle everywhere. David wasn't certain what kind of medicine Homer had practiced, but he had a feeling that the old boy would like to play doctor with Gran. Homer was distinguished-looking, with a full head of gray hair and a thin moustache. He resembled an aging version of Clark Gable and his southern manners spoke of a genteel life.

The parking lot at the hospital was already covered with a light blanket of snow, and the Visitor Parking sign glowed dimly in the darkness. Grabbing a small bouquet of flowers off the passenger seat, David headed inside to visit Gran.

Her room was cheerily adorned with cards, flower arrangements and, unfortunately for David, people. Homer and Rose sat in chairs beside her bed, watching television. This should be interesting. Now Gran would have someone to help her meddle in his love life. Between the three of them, they should have him squared away in no time.

"David Barclay! As I live and breathe, how did you make it to Sea Grove in this weather? It's not fit for man nor beast out there!" Rose struggled to extricate herself from her form-fitting chair.

"Hi, Rose. You're looking beautiful, as always." David kissed her chubby pink cheek as she dragged his leather jacket off.

"David, honey, come in!" Abigail's thin voice floated out to him from somewhere amid her jungle of plants and flowers.

"Good to see you, Dr. Penwalt," David said, grasping his hand as Homer rose to greet him.

"Hello, David, my boy. We were just looking for the weather report." Homer stepped over to the TV and turned down the volume.

Abigail held out her arms to David. "You look wonderful, all things considered. Sit down over here by me and tell me how you're doing." She patted the edge of her hospital bed. It was just like her to throw the spotlight on him. Gran wasn't one to complain, unless it was about the fact that he wasn't married—yet. She still had high hopes for him.

"Fine, Gran. Never better." He hugged his grandmother gently, and eased his large frame somewhat awkwardly down on the end of the bed. "How are you feeling?" Da-

vid was pleased to note that her color was much better than
the last time he'd visited.

"Good enough to come after you if you're not eating
right," she told him. Abigail's sharp eyes searched his face.
"You're looking skinny. Are you getting enough to eat?"

David sighed. Here we go, he thought. Let the inquisi-
tion begin. "Yes, Gran, I'm eating well. Three squares a
day."

"Square what? Are you getting enough exercise?"

He nodded. "I work out almost every day."

"Well, don't overdo it."

David rolled his eyes. Homer patted him sympathetically
on the back. "He looks fine to me, Abby. So, how goes the
law practice, David? Any big cases coming up?"

"Just the usual, Homer. Alimony, child support, cus-
tody battles."

Abigail eyed her grandson morosely. "That's so sad. I
don't know how you do it. All those poor people wanting
out of their marriages. Why? I just don't understand it.
Marriage is one of the happiest things that can happen to a
person."

"Well, Gran, from what I can see, it's not all it's cracked
up to be. My parents are a perfect example of that." David's eyes sparked painfully at the memory of his mother's
and father's constant bickering.

"That doesn't count. Your parents were a couple of selfish ninnies, may they rest in peace. If they'd lived longer,
they might have seen the light. People just don't try anymore." Abigail's hand fluttered over her heart, and her eyes
grew bright. "Marrying Bertrand Barclay was the best thing
I ever did. You wouldn't even be here if I hadn't."

David reached over to take her hand. "I know, Gran, and
I'm glad you did. But marriage isn't for everyone. Like me,
for example. I'm very happy without the hassle and expense I see my clients go through." The muffled drone of the
TV set seemed to echo in the suddenly quiet room.

Rose finally broke the silence. "I'll just go see what's keeping your dinner, Abby," she announced, squeezing past Homer on her way out the door.

Adjusting his chair, Homer spoke, his expression thoughtful. "You know, David, I never married. Had a couple of chances, but for one reason or another, never made it to the altar. First the war, then school, of course, and then my practice." He picked up his pipe but, mindful of where he was, didn't light it. "Just never seemed to be the right time. Kind of like you." Scratching his lower lip with the stem of his pipe, he continued.

"I had my work and my friends. One or two of them were ladies, you see." He chuckled. "But, as I recollect, none of them really had what it took. You know, that special spark. Electricity, if you will. That is, of course, until I met your grandmother." Abigail sniffed and colored slightly. "But, unfortunately for me, she was taken. As I got older, I always had the feeling that I missed out on something quite wonderful."

David set his elbows on his knees and leaned forward. "Well, how about it, Gran? Are you thinking about tying the knot again?"

"We're not talking about me, young man," she snapped. "So don't try to change the subject. Are you dating anyone?"

"At the moment no." David thought back to earlier that afternoon, when he'd shaken the hand of the sexy, raven-haired beauty across the hall. Talk about sparks. Homer ought to try a handshake or two with that one. Oh, hell. She was probably taken. They usually were. And if they weren't, they generally had problems he had no interest in solving. Still, there had definitely been something between them. He knew she'd felt it, too. Her large, expressive blue eyes had given her away. She had curves in all the right places. Looked like she was in pretty good shape. Legs so long, they seemed to go on for—

"David?"

He shifted uncomfortably in his chair. The room had suddenly grown stiflingly hot. What on earth was he thinking, sitting here fantasizing in front of Gran and Homer?

"I'm sorry, Gran, did you say something?"

Abigail and Homer exchanged glances. "Homer asked if you'd like a glass of water. You're looking flushed."

"Oh, no, thanks, Homer." He shook his head. "So, Gran, now that you're feeling better, how long till they spring you?"

"Not soon enough for me. I'm living on borrowed time. Which, by the way, is why I'm so anxious to see you settle down and start a family. It's just ridiculous that all the family you have in the world is an old granny with one foot on a roller skate and the other in a coffin."

Sadness filled David's eyes as he looked at the wonderful woman who had given him so much. He hated it when she talked about dying, or going to be with Bertie, as she liked to put it. She was the only real family he had, and he just couldn't envision life without Abigail.

Suddenly he felt strangely depressed. *Get ahold of yourself, man,* he commanded himself. You're only thirty-one years old. And Abigail's fine. Just fine.

Rose arrived with the dinner tray, and the small room became a windmill of activity as she leaned over Abigail plumping, fluffing, pouring, spooning, fanning and clucking.

"All right now, all set. Abby, will you say grace?"

"Yes, Rose, thank you." Gran bowed her head and began. "Lord, thank you for the food, friends, and, of course family... what's left of it, that is, Lord." She shot a quick glance at David. "And, Lord, please take care of my grandson, bring him happiness and a loving family when I'm gone. Amen."

"Amen," Rose and Homer echoed.

Great, thought David. *Now I don't stand a chance.*

"Would you like something to eat, David?" Rose asked hopefully. "The hospital dietitian is a friend of mine."

"Oh, no, thank you, Rose. I have to watch my boyish figure." He leaned back on the bed and stretched, his muscles flexing and moving under his cotton shirt.

"Oh, pshaw. Look at you. You're hard as a rock." Rose reached over and playfully squeezed his large bicep.

David chuckled and patted her meaty arm. "What time is it, Homer? I should probably get back before they start closing the roads."

Homer looked at his watch, humming thoughtfully. "Why, it's nearly eleven o'clock. Imagine that."

"Let's watch the weather report and see how bad all this storm stuff is," Abigail commanded. Rose picked up the remote control and adjusted the volume.

While she waited for the weatherman, Abigail took up the threads of the conversation where she'd left off during her meal. His love life. Or lack thereof. "So tell me, David. What ever happened to Mariette, or Margaret, or whoever she was?"

"Martina. She got a partnership with a law firm in New York."

"So, I take it you're not seeing her anymore?" Abigail looked so disappointed, he hated to tell her the truth.

"No, Gran." David had been relieved when Martina packed up and went east. She hadn't been his type. No sparkle. No sizzle. No electricity.

Again he thought back to his new neighbor. He replayed that simple handshake in his mind. Her cheeks had been pink from the cold, and her long, wavy jet-black hair had had sparkly drops of water in it where the snow had melted. Her full lips had looked so kissable. He liked the way she sort of chewed her lower lip when she was flustered.

What was it about that simple handshake that had had him breathing so hard as he rode the elevator to the basement? The current that had run between their hands each time he touched her had been so strong it could have powered a light bulb.

It must have something to do with her voice. Low and sexy, it oozed sensuality. What was it she'd said? She was rehearsing for a play. He'd have to go see her in that, if it meant he could listen to her talk for a couple of hours. The sound reverberated in his memory. If he thought hard enough, he could almost hear it here in the room with him. It seemed to be saying, "Our top story tonight, heavy snowstorms headed for the Seattle area, more right after this..." Then it seemed to discuss feminine hygiene products. No, that wasn't her voice. That was a commercial. He was beginning to hear things.

"Here we go, David. Listen! She's talking about your storm." Abigail leaned toward the television set. "I like her." She pointed at the screen. "She's the best on this channel. That other one they have, what's her name? Edna Addison? She's a dolt. Now, *this* one, Lauren Wills, she's sharp as a tack. And about the prettiest thing going. She puts that poor Edna to shame."

Lauren Wills? Where had he heard that name? David leaned forward on the bed to get a closer look at the television screen. That name. That voice. That sexy, electric voice.

"She's my neighbor!"

Chapter Two

Aⅼl three gray heads turned to stare at David at the same time.

"Lauren Wills is your *neighbor?*" Abigail echoed. "My, my, how about that?"

"You lucky dog! She's charming," Homer put in.

Yes. How about that? Lauren Wills from the eleven-o'clock news was his neighbor. When did she ever have time to rehearse for a play? Her boyfriend or husband must suffer.

"She's not married." Abigail seemed to be reading his mind. "No, never has been, either. *Seattle Weekly* did a cover story on her almost a month ago. She's a wonderful person, really. So giving. So kind. Yes, it told all about her. Maybe I still have it here in this pile of magazines." She leaned over and began digging through the stack on her nightstand.

Homer, who'd been paying attention to the news report, spoke up. "Well, David, you'll be all right if you want to make a run for it. The snow's let up some. Supposed to be back with a vengeance tomorrow. Which reminds me. I'd better go see about putting some tire chains on the old bike.''

Were there such things? David wondered. "I'll take you and your bike home in the Jeep, Homer.''

"Now there's a fine idea. I'll go get ready.''

"Don't be a stranger now, honey,'' Rose said as she straightened the collar on his jacket after she helped him on with it. A smothering hug and an enthusiastic kiss later, he was ready to leave.

"Here it is, David. Here's that article on Lauren Wills. I knew I had it here somewhere. Isn't that a lovely picture of her?'' Abigail thrust the article into his hands.

He studied the cover of the *Seattle Weekly* with interest. The caption read Local Celebrity Lauren Wills Sails for Charity. A smiling Lauren was pictured leaning against the railing of a large sailboat. She was wearing a bikini and a gauzy white overwrap that did little to hide her perfect body. Better than I thought, he mused. She *did* work out. Her yachting cap was angled jauntily, and the sun kissed her high cheekbones as she looked down at the camera through her long, dark lashes.

Homer came back in from the parking lot and shook the snow out of his hair. "All set.''

"Goodbye, you two.'' Abigail gently hugged and kissed each of them as they bent over her bed. "Drive carefully, just like I taught you now, son. And, David, tell Lauren Wills that your feeble old grandmother would love to have her autograph.''

Rose, Homer and Abigail all exchanged meaningful glances. *Now what was that all about?* They were like three little kids when it came to interfering in his life.

"Okay, Gran. When and *if* I ever see her again.'' Abigail looked crestfallen. "Okay, okay, I'll try,'' he said, sighing, and she perked up considerably. "Bye you two, and keep her out of trouble, Rose.''

Later that night, David lay across his bed and fished the article Abigail had given him out of his jacket pocket. It was already after one in the morning. The snow had really started coming down by the time he pulled into the underground parking lot in his building. Good thing tomorrow was Saturday. He could just stay home and catch up on his paperwork.

Smoothing the wrinkles out of the magazine, he turned the pages until he found the cover story. Inside, there were more black-and-white pictures of her. One with other local celebrities, working on the charity regatta for the Benedictine Home for the Aging. Another shot showed Lauren at the anchor desk during a newscast. He quickly scanned the article.

She was twenty-nine years old, single, born and raised in the Seattle area, mother Charlotte, father Jack, one eighteen-year-old brother, Zach. Degree in broadcast journalism, very career-minded, loved sports, involved in a number of charitable organizations.

The article went on, and David could see why Gran was so impressed. But the story said nothing about how sexy her handshake was. Maybe she hadn't shaken hands with the guy who wrote this article, he thought drowsily. Good. He liked a woman who didn't shake hands with just anyone. He yawned broadly and rolled over on top of the cover picture of Lauren. He liked her hands. Her sexy, electric hands. They were so... David's breathing deepened as he began to sleep.

Lauren slowly woke to a freezing-cold room. She had forgotten to set the thermostat. *I don't want to get up,* she thought as an icy-cold paw batted her tentatively on the cheek.

"Go away, Hairball," she mumbled. "Go make some coffee."

Hairball had other ideas. She listened to him chewing on her tangled hair for a moment and sighed. "Okay, I get the picture. You're hungry."

Throwing back the covers, she padded across the floor to the window. The world had been covered in a thick white blanket. Luckily, today was Saturday. She could just stay home and catch up on her paperwork.

Shivering, Lauren grabbed her bathrobe off the bed and went into the living room to turn on the heat. Hairball dodged and weaved between her legs, and finally, in irritation, she scooped him up.

"Come here, you. Keep me warm." The tiger-striped tabby purred loudly and rammed his head into her neck. "We have messages, Hairy," she said, glancing at her phone machine. "Who's been calling you? You don't have a new girlfriend, too, do you?" Hairball struggled to get out of her arms. "Men." She harrumphed as she put on a pot of coffee and fed the cat.

The air was considerably warmer by the time she wandered into her large, art deco bathroom. Turning the shower on, she stared at her reflection in the mirror while she waited for the water to heat.

Dark circles shadowed her eyes. No wonder. It had been after one o'clock when she finally pulled into the garage last night.

The hot water was soothing, and rivers of shampoo lather ran down her back and into the drain. For hours after she'd gone to bed, she'd lain awake and mulled over her breakup with Joe.

"I'll bet good old Joe hasn't lost any sleep over me." She bit the words out angrily and slammed the shower off. Why was she torturing herself with images of Joe and Tanya? She didn't really want him any more than he seemed to want her.

Lauren stepped out of the shower and dried off with a huge, fluffy bath sheet. The blow dryer threw her naturally wavy hair into a dark, wild mane. Deftly she applied her makeup with a practiced hand. Well, at least Hairball would be impressed with her appearance. Besides, she already felt better. Standing inside her walk-in closet, she tried to decide what to wear. Something warm. The pale pink angora sweater was good, and her beat-up old jeans with holes in all the right places.

She grabbed her slippers and headed into her spacious, elegant living room. It was straight out of *House Beautiful*. Lauren loved antiques. She and Polly had combed the entire Seattle area for months, searching for just the right pieces. Tasteful flower arrangements, paintings and sculptures complemented the muted tones she'd chosen for her walls and drapes.

"Let's see who called us, Hairy," she said, stepping over him and pouring herself a cup of coffee. The sound of her greeting filled the room.

Hairball cocked an inquisitive ear in the direction of the sound.

"You have reached the newsroom. Please file your story at the deadline." *Time to change the greeting,* she thought. Too corny. Polly had talked her into that one. The machine beeped and played three messages—one from her mother, one from Edna Addison at the station, and one from Polly. Deciding there was no time like the present, she dialed the station.

Edna wondered if they could meet on Monday to discuss Lauren's vacation at Christmas. She had two weeks that she had to use or lose, and Edna had been assigned to hold down the fort in her absence. Lauren and Joe had toyed with the idea of going to the Bahamas. That was a moot point now, she thought grumpily as she jabbed at the phone, punching in her mother's number.

Lauren hadn't seen her family for nearly a month, so she promised to have dinner with her mom and dad as soon as the weather permitted. Lastly, she called Polly.

"Pol, it's me, Lauren." She took a sip of her steaming coffee and settled back on her couch for a good chat. "I'm glad you're home."

"Where else would I be in this weather? I'm up to my elbows in Popsicle sticks and glue. So, how are you? Depressed?" she asked sympathetically.

"Not depressed, really. More mad than anything." It was too soon to be sure how she felt.

"That's . . . good." Polly had expected Lauren to be in tears. "You're not in denial or anything, are you?" she asked worriedly.

"No, I don't think so." Having finished his meal, Hairball jumped into Lauren's lap and began to wrestle with the phone cord. "I'm sure there are hundreds of painful things I haven't even thought of, but right now I'm most concerned about finding a date to the Christmas ball."

"Joe's taking Tanya?"

"Yes."

"The slime."

Lauren laughed. She could just see her diminutive friend gearing up for a fight. With her riot of auburn curls, Polly sometimes reminded Lauren of a lioness defending her cub. It was hard to believe Polly taught kindergarten. She was hardly bigger than her students.

"What does he see in that bimbo? You know, you could always go with Gus and me. He'll be playing with the jazz band. At least you wouldn't have to be alone. Ohhh!" Polly groaned, and Lauren could hear the clatter of something crashing in the background. "My birdhouse," she explained sadly.

"Polly, you don't know any fabulously handsome single guys who'd want to go to the ball, do you?"

"Only the guys in Gus's band, and I don't know if you'd call any of them fabulously handsome. Not even cute, really. But they're good guys."

"No thanks. They'll probably be playing all night, anyway." Lauren hesitated. "Maybe I should ask that new guy across the hall. . . ."

Polly was instantly interested. "What new guy?"

Lauren took a deep breath. If she said it out loud, she might have to act on it, and she didn't know if she was prepared for that.

"Oh, nothing. He's probably married. All the good ones are."

"What nothing? Who nothing?" Polly could be like a pit bull when she wanted information.

Lauren giggled and pushed the cat onto the floor. "I've got a new neighbor, and he seems . . . nice."

"What do you mean, *nice?* Tell Aunt Polly all about him."

"Well . . . he's gorgeous. He's tall, dark and handsome, with a body that won't quit. Big arms and chest, but slim, really. And he has the cutest dimple in his left cheek when he smiles. He's funny. Great hair, too. He wears it kind of feathered in the front, and longish in the back. It's real thick and wavy. And he has wonderful hands." Her voice was growing dreamy.

"Man, have you gone off the deep end, or what?"

Lauren sat up and pulled her legs up under her. "No, no, no. You know I don't have time for a serious relationship. And it's not like I'm on the rebound from that snake Joe, or anything. It's just . . . I don't know how to explain it."

"He sure sounds good."

"He *would* be the perfect revenge. Anyway, if he's not married, maybe I'll work up the nerve to ask him to the mayor's Christmas ball. I could show old Joe-baby and the Tanster that I have a life. Kind of . . ."

"Sounds like you have it all figured out. Just be careful," Polly warned. "You don't want to get hurt or anything."

"Hey, this is me you're talking to. Sensible, levelheaded, power-driven Lauren. I won't let it get out of control. Ha! Listen to me! What if he says no?"

"I guess you won't know if you don't ask. You should see this birdhouse. It's a scream. Keep me posted on your progress with the neighbor," Polly instructed her. "I'll probably see you Monday or Tuesday, if it ever stops snowing. We've got another big storm coming soon." Another loud crash. "Oops, gotta go."

Hanging up the phone, she heard the dull thud of the newspaper hitting her front door. Well, that would kill some time, she thought, and shuffled to her door.

* * *

David woke up, rolled over, stretched and yawned. What was stuck to his stomach? He opened one eye halfway, peered down over his lightly furred pectorals and slowly peeled Lauren's picture off his body.

"Mmm... Good morning, gorgeous. Was it as good for you as it was for me?" He grinned at her smiling face. What a babe.

Sitting up, he swung his legs over the side of his bed. He ran his hand through his thick, dark hair and stood up. Stretching and scratching, he walked over to the window. Damn. Though it looked pretty, the snow meant a lot of work. Oh, well. I should do some laundry today, he thought as he stepped into the shower.

"I gotta be me...I gotta dee dee...what else dee dee dee but dee dee am..." he bellowed as he lathered up and rinsed his body. "Ba dee dee dee dum, ba dee dee dee dum, but what—" he finished with a flourish as he turned the water off—"I am!"

Grabbing a towel off the floor, David briskly dried himself, quickly shaved and headed to his closet. The Sonics were playing today, he thought, pulling an old football jersey out of another pile of clothes. Smelling it, he decided it would pass and stretched it on over his head. He pulled on a faded pair of jeans and went to the kitchen to make coffee.

The aroma of fresh-perked java followed him into his sparsely furnished living room. David believed in the uncluttered approach to decor. It was easier to dust that way. Gray walls, gray carpet, white woodwork, black modular furniture, and a couple of colorful modern paintings thrown in for good measure. Austere, but lived-in. Okay, messy. So he was no housekeeper—big deal.

He picked up the phone and punched in the Sea Grove Community Hospital's number. "Dee dee dee dee da..." he hummed softly as he listened to it ring. That was strange. No answer. He let it ring more than a dozen times, then hung up. He'd try Homer's. David pulled his organizer out of his briefcase and looked under *P* in its directory. Pen-walt, Dr. Homer. He picked up the phone again and punched the number in. Again it rang over a dozen times with no answer. Strange. Well, he'd try later.

David switched on the television and looked for the game. His paperwork could wait. It was just starting when a female voice came on and announced a special report.

It turned out to be a local warning about a series of storms coming later in the week. Too bad it wasn't his sexy neighbor giving all the details. Maybe he should go next door and get his news up close and personal. That reminded him. He'd better go pick up his newspaper.

They opened their front doors and stepped into the hall-way at the same time.

"Hi," they said in unison, and then they both laughed.

She introduced herself again. "Lauren."

"David." He held his hand out. She took it. There it was *again!* David looked down at the floor in confusion. This was ridiculous, being electrified by a little handshake. This never happened to him. He was tough. He was cool. He was...speechless.

"Good morning." She smiled up at him bashfully. Little jolts of awareness still ran between their hands.

"Yes." His look was so piercing, Lauren suddenly felt naked. Slowly she pulled her hand from his, and she thought she caught a look of disappointment on his face. She noticed that he wasn't wearing a wedding ring, and wondered idly how she could bring the mayor's Christmas ball into the conversation. *Ask him!* the angel on her right shoulder screamed. *No! Not yet!* the angel on her left shoulder screamed. Lauren swallowed nervously.

David finally found his voice. "So, you're taking a break from rehearsing your play?"

"In a way, yes." She guessed forever was a break. A long break.

"You're even prettier in real life." David reddened when he realized he'd spoken out loud.

"Oh. You know, then."

She seemed embarrassed. She was cute when she was flushed. He felt like an idiot. She shouldn't be embarrassed, she should be proud.

"Yeah. I saw you last night. You're my grandmother's favorite. Mine, too," he added. Make that superidiot. What was he doing? Something about her flustered the hell out of him.

"That's nice." She blushed. "What do you do?"

"I'm an attorney."

She lifted an interested eyebrow. "What kind of law?"

"Divorce." He looked into her deep blue eyes.

"Mmm, hmm." She seemed impressed. Not disgusted. Maybe this wasn't so bad after all. "How's your grandmother feeling?"

It was ridiculous how much it pleased him that she had asked. "Fine. Improving every day."

"I'm so glad," she said, genuinely relieved.

Hairball chose that instant to streak through her door and pounce on his feet. Delighted to be free of the confines of Lauren's condo, he attacked David's toes with gusto. Throwing his forepaws around David's ankle, he rolled over onto his back as if he were trying to flip the man.

"Hey, hey, hey, little tiger. I need those!" David burst out laughing. Picking up his paper and the bundle of fur, he rubbed the cat's head. Hairball purred loudly, loving the attention. He wriggled around in ecstasy, knocking the newspaper out of David's arms. It hit the floor with a startling smack. Scrambling up David's chest in terror, the frightened animal wrapped itself around his neck, clinging for dear life.

"Ouch!" David tried unsuccessfully to pry the paralyzed feline from his body. Hairy dug in deeper, his ears flat, his tail nervously slapping David in the face.

Lauren was mortified. "Bad boy!" she cried, pulling the reluctant animal, toenail by toenail, off his port in the storm. "I'm so sorry! Did he hurt you?"

"No, he was just playing," David asserted manfully. Actually, it hurt like hell. He felt like a human pincushion.

Hairball, looking remorseful, reached out a tentative paw from Lauren's arms, as if to say he was sorry.

"No, look." Lauren pointed at the slashes in his football jersey.

"This old thing? Don't worry about it."

She shook her head quickly, still pointing. "You're bleeding!"

"Oh?" David tucked in his chin and peered down at his chest. She was right, he was bleeding.

"Why don't you come inside? I have some of that orange stuff that stings like the devil."

"That's okay, I'll live." He was really feeling foolish now.

"Please? I insist. It's the least I can do. Besides—" she looked up at him and grinned "—if it gets infected, you could sue me."

How could he resist her large, pleading blue eyes. "That's a novel idea," he mused, returning her grin. "Usually I'm busy suing for divorce."

Opening her front door, she picked up her paper and laughed. "That won't be necessary. He's not married."

"Who?"

"Hairball." Lauren could have just died. First her cat mauls him, then . . .

"Hairball? That's disgusting!" He looked at the fat lump of hair in amusement. "What did you do to deserve that name? Don't answer that," he commanded, following Lauren into her apartment.

Lauren pushed the cat into her living room and closed the door behind David.

"Nice," he commented appreciatively, surveying her lovely home.

"Thanks," she murmured as she slipped past him and headed toward her bathroom. Quickly searching her medicine cabinet, she grabbed some iodine, bandages, a damp cloth and a bottle of aspirin. She was no nurse, but she felt confident she could handle a few scratches without fainting. Until she reached her living room. There she found Michelangelo's *David,* standing naked from the waist up, cleaning his wounds with his battered shirt. She froze, staring helplessly, and sucked in her breath.

How on earth was she supposed to bandage *that?* Her hands were trembling so badly, she nearly dropped her supplies.

"Here—here you go," she stammered, thrusting her armload at him.

Struggling to balance everything, David lifted his eyebrows in a curious glance. "Blood make you queasy?" he asked, setting everything down on her coffee table. He dabbed gingerly at his injuries, while Lauren watched in fascination.

"Could you . . . open that for me?" He nodded at the iodine bottle.

Lauren eyed the bottle with misgivings, "Um, sure." Twisting off the cap, she dipped the brush into the orange liquid and held it out to him.

He had no sooner stemmed the trickle on one scratch than another began to drip. He needed three hands. Moving closer to her, he asked, "Would you mind?" and gestured toward the marks across his powerful chest and abdomen. "Be gentle with me," he said as she studied his scratches with apprehension. He winced as she carefully painted the medicine first on one scratch, then on another, until he was a road map of orange highways and byways.

"Good heavens." She giggled nervously. "You look like you've just been in the shoot-out at the OK Corral."

"I'm beginning to think we need a tourniquet," he joked, studying the mess on his chest.

That made her laugh harder. "That's a little drastic," she told him, choking. Taking the washcloth out of his hand, she swiped at the few remaining drips.

His skin was so warm. So smooth and so soft. It was ironic that something could be so soft and so hard at the same time. The muscles that ran beneath her fingertips were like steel bands. He made her feel small and fragile, standing there next to him, which was odd, considering how tall she was. But he was taller and stronger and more powerful.

The laughter died on her lips, and she looked up to find him watching her hands on his chest. Hastily she wadded up the cloth and tossed it on the table.

"You—" she cleared her throat "—you seem to have stopped bleeding." She picked up the bandages uncertainly.

"I think you're right. I'll skip the bandages, if you don't mind. Taking them off could be painful." He displayed the dimple in his left cheek, and Lauren could feel her insides beginning to churn.

That's good, she thought in relief. She didn't think any more contact with his naked chest was such a bright idea.

David lifted his blood-spattered jersey off the coffee table and carefully pulled it on over his wounds.

She handed his newspaper to him. "I hear we're in for some more snow, toward the end of next week."

"Yeah, this last storm was unusual for this time of year. According to this, we'll probably be able to make it to work by Monday, but by the weekend we'll most likely be snowbound again." David held the weather section out for her to see. He was standing so close she could smell his after-shave. It smelled sexy, like him.

"It sure looks that way. I kind of like it. The snow, I mean. It makes everything feel sort of cozy," she said. His expression was unreadable as he looked down at her. *That was a dumb thing to say,* she thought. *Now he probably thinks I want to get cozy with him. I'm such an idiot.*

"Well," he said, backing toward her door, "I should probably let you get back to rehearsing. Break a leg."

"Pardon?"

"Your play."

"Oh, right." She smiled guiltily. "Again, I'm so sorry about Hairy. He was just scared."

"Forget it. The way I look at it, we're even. I still feel bad about knocking you over yesterday. And hey, if you need anything, the two of us being snowbound and all, just come get me." He stepped into the hallway and opened his door.

"Thanks, I will." She couldn't find the words to ask about the ball. Maybe next time.

Their eyes locked for a heart-stopping moment. Each of them was wondering what the other was thinking. "Bye," they said in unison, and laughed. Their doors closed together.

It continued to snow most of the day. David had been dialing Abigail and Homer on and off all day, and the later it got, the more worried he became. He wished Homer'd use the answering machine he'd gotten him last Christmas. At least then he could leave a message. He slammed down the phone in frustration and dialed the operator.

A nasal voice buzzed across the line. "This is the operator. May I help you?"

"Yes. Are you able to tell if the phone lines are down in a certain area?"

She sighed noisily in his ear. "Honey, where *aren't* the phone lines down? Where are you trying to call?"

"Sea Grove." David gave her Abigail's number at the hospital. Then he threw in Homer's for good measure.

"One moment, please." Elevator music filled the headset.

While David was waiting, he tried to think of reasons to be out in the hallway without looking like he was loitering. He couldn't believe what a clod he'd been earlier. Usually, when it came to women, he was sophisticated. Clever. Suave, even. He wanted a chance to prove that to her. *I can't believe I told her she was prettier in real life! What a clown!* he thought, pounding his forehead with the palm of his hand.

"Sir?" Her voice jolted him back to reality.

"Yes?"

"I tried both numbers and got no answer. Then I called our dispatch department. They say they've heard that there are outages in that area, and it will probably be several days before all the lines are back up again. Sometimes it takes a while to restore service in small rural areas like Sea Grove. Give it a couple of days."

"I will. Thank you." David dropped the handset into the phone's cradle. That answered that. At least he could stop worrying about Abigail. No news was good news.

No amount of loitering in the hallway produced another meeting with Lauren that weekend, much to his disappointment. She must have been rehearsing her play. He filled his time by sweeping his spotless doorway, changing a perfectly good light bulb and puttying a nail hole. Finally, disgusted with himself, he finished the paperwork on his latest case—when he could concentrate on it. A leggy, raven-haired fantasy kept intruding on his progress. He had to force himself to stop thinking about her. He was a divorce lawyer, for crying out loud. He knew better than to want any kind of romantic involvement. It usually went sour. Like his parents'.

Sunday brought light snow showers till noon, when it finally began to warm up. By Monday morning, the roads were clear enough for David to make it to work, and the day passed in a whirlwind of phone calls and meetings. He tried dialing Abigail, to no avail. He figured the lines were still out.

By Tuesday evening, he was really starting to worry about Abigail. Maybe he should drive out there, he thought. The next storm wasn't due till Friday, and he could probably make it without too much trouble. He was just considering the idea when his phone rang.

"David? It's Rose. David, honey?" Rose sounded really strange. Flustered and nervous. "David, it's your grandmother. She's..." She was clearly searching for the right words. "She's had another attack."

Chapter Three

David's world felt as if it were spinning out of control. White as a sheet, he began to sweat and shiver. Fearing his legs would give out, he sank down on the arm of his couch.

"Rose, calm down, and just tell me what's going on." He sounded steadier than he felt.

"It happened just after you left," Rose explained. "Honey, I wanted to call you sooner, but . . ."

"I know, the lines were down. I've been trying to get through to you for four days. How is she? Is she all right? Do you want me to come up now?"

David's rapid-fire questions rendered Rose silent for a moment. Then she said, "She is going to be fine. Just fine. The doctor has her on stronger heart medication now, and he says she is responding well. In fact, they say she can go home this weekend."

"Oh, thank God." David exhaled the breath he'd been holding while Rose answered his questions.

"Now, David, there's more. It seems when she had the attack, she lost consciousness for a while. When she's awake . . . she's a little dingy."

"How dingy?" He slid off the couch's arm onto its seat.

"Very dingy."

"Very dingy?"

"Very, *very* dingy." Rose cleared her throat. "I don't really understand all the medical ins and outs, honey. But the bottom line seems to be that when she had her heart problem, there was some blood loss to the brain, and she's sort of fuzzy on some details. Homer can explain it all to you, I'm sure."

"What do you mean, 'fuzzy'?" David didn't like the sound of this one bit.

"Well, she doesn't recognize me, and she thinks Homer is your grandpa Bertie. But don't worry too much, now, the doctor seems to think her condition is temporary. She should bounce back to her old self sooner or later."

Rose paused. She was beginning to sound flustered. "Now, David, I've got a small problem I need your help with. My daughter Gloria, you remember her—the one in Arizona? She's having her first baby soon, maybe as early as next week, and she wants me to come down and help out. I was hoping Abigail would be okay alone, but she's so out of it..."

David summed up what Rose was trying to say. "You need someone to take care of Gran while you're gone."

"Yes! That's right. I don't want to be any trouble, and I know you have to work, but I was thinking maybe she could stay with you for a while, just till I get back, of course."

David's mind raced. "Okay. I suppose that would be fine, Rose, if you're *sure* she's all right to travel. I could bring a lot of my paperwork home, and make client calls from here. I guess I could get someone to stay with her when I have to leave. What about her doctor? Her medicine?"

Rose seemed to think about that for a second. "Homer got all of her prescriptions filled, and they should last for over a month. And her doctor says physically she's fine, as long as she takes her pills, and stays calm."

Thank heavens for Rose and Homer, David thought gratefully. "Rose, when do you want me to come up? I could leave right now. The roads are still clear."

"Oh, that's really not necessary." Rose assured him. "I'll stay here at the hospital with her for the rest of the week. I don't have to leave for Gloria's till Saturday afternoon. I've been watching the long-range weather forecasts, and there isn't supposed to be another snowstorm until Sunday. I'm so glad. I'm such a nervous flier."

"Is she there now, Rose? Can I talk to her?"

"Oh, she's here all right, but she's asleep. No sense wasting time talking to her, either. She's still pretty confused. You can see her this weekend. Homer and I will bring her to your place."

"Okay," David said reluctantly. "I'll fix up the spare room for her, and you can bring her down Saturday morning. You'll get her all packed up?"

"Yes, dear. And Saturday morning will be fine. Around nine."

"Saturday it is, then, around nine. And, Rose, if there is any change in her condition—I mean *any* change—call me."

"I'll have Homer tell you everything Abby's doctor says Saturday morning. She just needs a lot of rest and quiet. The doctor says to treat her with kid gloves till she's up to snuff in the head. You know, no shocks to the heart. You'll do just fine." Rose sounded much more confident than David felt.

"I guess so. Thanks for calling, Rose. You're terrific."

"Pshaw. It's nothing, I assure you. I'll see you Saturday, honey. And thanks for helping out. Bye-bye."

"Call me with any news, Rose. Bye." David stared at the receiver in his hand for a second before he hung up. Gran had been sick, and he hadn't even known. He shook his head in disbelief. How could it all have happened so fast? Fear gripped him as he realized that someday it would all happen for real. Abigail would be gone, and he would be alone.

I sure hope I'm up to this nursing bit, he thought as he got off the couch and headed for bed. *Just how dingy was she?*

Lauren had an amazingly productive week, rushing to get everything done before she left for her two-week vacation the following Monday. She and Edna ironed out a lot of last-minute details over dinner Monday night, before the eleven-o'clock show.

After the five-o'clock news show Tuesday evening, Lauren drove out to South Seattle and had dinner at Polly's place. Her friend was dying to hear more about David.

"So, have you seen him again since Hairball assaulted him?"

Lauren cringed. "No. I kept going out into the hall for all kinds of dumb reasons, but he was never there. I'm sure he's busy. He doesn't have time to stand around loitering in his doorway," she said contritely.

"He sounds wonderful. When do I get to see him?"

"I don't know, Pol." Lauren leaned back in her chair and threw her crumpled napkin on her plate. "Want to come over and hang out in the hallway with me?"

"Sure. If you're going to lasso this little dogie in time for the ball, you'd better do something."

"You're right. Next time I see him, I'll ask him for sure."

Thursday night, Lauren ran home to change before she went out to a late dinner with her family. The wool business suit she'd worn on the air at five was scratchy, so she changed into a soft white jersey sweater dress that fitted her like a glove. The large shoulder pads accentuated her tiny waist, and the short hem line showed off her slender, shapely legs. In the bathroom, she freshened her lipstick and piled her hair loosely on top of her head with a large white clip.

Grabbing her clutch purse, keys and coat, she turned out the lights and patted Hairball on his pudgy stomach.

"Be a good kitty and fend off any intruders, huh, Hairy?"

"Meah," Hairball answered.

"And no clawing the furniture."

"Meoo." He grabbed his tail and bit it. Lauren could swear sometimes he said "yeah" and "no." Maybe she was turning into one of those old maids who talked to their cats. *Nah*, she thought, as she walked into her hallway and locked her front door.

A tired voice came from behind her. "Hi."

"Uh, hi yourself," she said, turning to face the speaker. Her heart skipped a beat, and a little thrill shivered up her spine. It was him. He looked wonderful, but beat. How did he do it? How could anyone who looked so good in a leather jacket and tight Levi's look this great in a gray pinstripe suit? His expensive tie matched the suspenders he wore over a crisply starched white shirt. A gray overcoat was slung casually over his shoulder, and the beginnings of a five-o'clock shadow darkened his jaw.

"Going out on a date?" he asked nonchalantly. He seemed vaguely depressed.

"Yes. I mean, no." She laughed. "Yes to going out. No, not on a date. I'm having dinner with my family."

"Oh. Have a good time." His eyes held hers for a moment, and he smiled slowly.

"How's your chest?" *Damn. That didn't sound right.*

His smile deepened. "Better."

"How are *you* doing?" There was concern in Lauren's voice.

"Ah, well now, that's a long story. I'm . . ." He paused, and unconsciously reached up to pull a strand of hair away from her mouth. His hand lightly brushed her cheek. A current of excitement ran from Lauren's face to the pit of her stomach. Something about David reminded her of those electric eels in the Seattle aquarium. ". . . not good," he continued and let his hand drop.

"Is there anything I can do?" *Climb a mountain? Ford a stream?* She meant it. Right now she would do anything to see that dimple again.

"No, not really." His upper lip lifted slowly to reveal his perfect white teeth. It was a sad smile.

"Well, if you think of anything..." her voice trailed off. She supposed that now was not the time to bring up the dance.

"There is one thing, maybe." He looked hopeful. "My grandmother's had another heart attack, and she's not herself."

"I'm so sorry," Lauren murmured in sympathy.

"Yeah, me, too," he said wistfully. "Anyway, she asked me... Oh, this is embarrassing." He ran his fingers through his hair and rubbed the back of his neck. The gesture was endearing, and Lauren's heart went out to him.

"Don't be embarrassed. It can't be that bad." Lauren grinned. "I don't do windows," she joked, trying to lighten his mood.

"No, no, nothing like that. I told her you were my neighbor, so she asked me to get your autograph," he finished in a rush. "I know, it's dumb, but she thinks you're great. Not dumb that she thinks you're great, of course, but..."

"I'm flattered," she said sincerely. "I have some press photos at work. I'll get one for you tomorrow and give it to you this weekend. You can bring it to her."

He was relieved. "Oh, that would be nice. She's going to be staying with me for a few days while she recovers. They tell me she's having trouble with her memory. I don't really know what to expect." He shrugged.

"Good luck," Lauren said earnestly. "I have to get going. I'll get that autograph for you by Saturday."

David unlocked his door and stepped inside. "Thanks," he said. He looked sincerely grateful. "Drive carefully," he added before he shut the door.

David threw his coat over the back of his couch and flopped into his recliner. *What a week,* he thought, loosening his tie. This latest divorce case was really getting him down. Just more fuel for his antimarriage fire.

And on top of everything else, there was Abigail. He leaned forward and pulled the phone off the coffee table by the couch. Rose picked up on the second ring.

"Hi, Rose. It's David. How goes the battle?" he asked tentatively. He wasn't up to coping with bad news.

"Hi, dearie. Fine, just fine. She's the same. Feeling better every day, but still confused. We told her she was going to stay with you a few days. She seemed happy about that. Then she asked who you were. I said, 'Why, he's your grandson, Abby.' Then she asked who Abby was."

David moaned as his temples began to throb. This was too much. "What am I going to do, Rose?"

"Just be your sweet self. She'll come around eventually. Is Saturday at nine still okay?" she asked.

"Yep. I don't need to buy a straitjacket or anything, do I?" David asked, making an attempt at humor.

"No, it's not as bad as that, honey. The doctor tells Homer he's seen this before. Usually the person snaps out of it in as little as a few weeks."

David took his tie off and formed a noose. "A few weeks, huh? This ought to be interesting. Okay, Rose. I'll see you Saturday."

David hung up thoughtfully. He'd see Lauren again on Saturday, too. If that didn't get him through the day, nothing would. She certainly was a knockout in that clingy white dress.

So she was going out with her family tonight. Good. So far no boyfriend. His dimple appeared for the first time that day.

The maître d' showed Lauren to the table where her family sat waiting. Jack Wills rose with a smile, and pulled a chair out for his daughter. Lauren's mother, Charlotte, leaned over and kissed her lightly on the cheek.

"Hi, sweetheart. You look lovely tonight." Charlotte smiled at her daughter, her bright blue eyes crinkling.

"Gets prettier every year. Just like her mother," her father boasted.

Zach looked pained. "Hey, guys, please. I have an image to maintain. What it is, homey." He tipped the brim of an invisible hat to his sister.

"Def and stupid, bro." They threw each other a high five across the table.

Jack and Charlotte looked at their children, then at each other, and shook their heads. Both of them appeared much younger than their early fifties. Jack was tall, solidly built, his sandy hair graying slightly. There were lines at the corners of his mouth and eyes, etched by years of good humor. Charlotte was a smaller version of her daughter, her dark hair stylishly short. Her large eyes twinkled with amusement.

"So, how is the world of television treating you, Lauren?" The pride in her father's voice was unmistakable.

"Very well, thanks, Dad. It's been hectic, but I love it. I'm taking a much-needed vacation next week." Lauren scanned the menu for something light.

Charlotte laid her menu down on the table. "Where are you going this time, honey?"

"Nowhere. I just want to stay home and veg out. No planes to catch, no bags to pack, no running here, there and everywhere." No palm trees, either, she thought, frowning at the menu.

"No way! What a bogus vacation! Lauren, you're gettin' to be a real bore." Zach leaned back on his chair's hind legs and beat a light tattoo on the table's edge with his silverware. His gold streaked hair hung wildly to his shoulders in a style that drove the girls crazy. It drove his parents crazy, too, but for different reasons.

"Zach, knock it off and sit up straight," Jack commanded the son who was already taller than he was. Zach made a halfhearted attempt at rearranging his posture.

After the waiter had taken their orders, her mother finally brought up the subject Lauren had been dreading— Joe.

"We've had a parting of the ways, so to speak." Lauren glanced at her mother, and back down to her long, lacquered nails.

Zach whooped. "The Joe-man flew the coup? *Hasta la bye-bye,* pretty boy!" he said, mockingly.

"Zach! That will be enough!" Her father covered his mouth with his napkin in an effort to suppress a grin.

"It's okay, Dad." Lauren smiled at her exuberant brother. Zach had never really warmed up to Joe, and the frigid feeling was mutual. Where Zach was extroverted, warm and funny, Joe had been cool and self-involved. No love lost there, she thought.

Charlotte reached over and took her daughter's hand. "I'm sorry, honey. Are you all right?"

"It hurts, but in a way, Mom, I'm almost relieved. Now that we're apart, I'm beginning to realize we didn't have much in common. Our relationship was just so... convenient." She paused as the waiter served their first course. "He's dating a model now. Tanya McDonald."

Zach smirked. "Tanya McDonald?"

"You know her?" Lauren asked.

"I've seen her. She's a stork. Lassie's head on a broom-handle body. Joe is such a squid," Zach said over a mouth-ful of food.

Jack was unsuccessful in his attempt to look sternly at his son. Their eyes met mischievously. "She's *that* bad?" he asked.

"Dad, she's an extraterrestrial."

Jack coughed until he turned bright red. Lauren reached over in distress and patted her dad on the back. No love lost between Jack and Joe, either, she surmised.

Charlotte eyed her son and husband quellingly. "Lauren, I sympathize with you. I know Joe was your... He was, well, he was convenient." Her family gave in to the laughter they'd all been holding back.

"What?" Charlotte's lips twitched.

"Oh, Mom." Lauren giggled. "It's okay. You don't have to defend him. It's over."

Jack mopped his forehead with his napkin and sighed. "Honey, anyone with your looks and talent, clearly inherited from me I might add—" he tossed this in Charlotte's direction "—doesn't need to waste a second feeling bad.

Why, I'm sure they're lining up outside your door already."

Lauren blushed furiously as thoughts of David came to mind.

"Oh, no," Zach groaned. "He's right! Look at her. Just when I was getting used to the idea of life without Zeus. Who is he?" he demanded.

Lauren feigned innocence. "Who's who?"

"The new Joe. The guy lined up outside your door."

"Nobody! Just a new neighbor. He's very nice." She had her entire family's rapt attention.

"Go on, honey. Tell us about him," Charlotte coaxed. So, for the rest of the meal, Lauren explained how they'd met and how his grandmother had taken ill.

"That's too bad about his grandmother. He sounds like a wonderful man." Charlotte put her arm around Lauren's shoulder as they prepared to leave the restaurant. "Not many young men would take on that kind of responsibility."

Zach chimed in. "That's for sure. When you and Dad start falling apart, you can call Lauren."

Saturday dawned crisp, bright and clear. Most of the snow from the previous week's storm had melted, leaving the roads clear for commuters. The weather forecasters were still predicting another storm, but it wasn't expected to arrive until late that night. David rushed around his apartment tidying up for Abigail. What couldn't be shoved under the bed or into a closet was thrown away. He'd sort it all out later, after Gran went home. How long would she be staying? he wondered. She could easily be with him through the holidays. That reminded him—he'd need to get a Christmas tree and decorations this year. He'd never bothered with that stuff before. Abigail always handled Christmas. But this Christmas had to be *very* special.

He could arrange for someone from his staff to come sit with Abigail while he got a tree and did some shopping. That should be no problem. He wouldn't be gone long. The past few days had been spent calling clients, organizing paperwork and briefing his staff so that he could work at home while she was there.

Promptly at nine o'clock, the doorbell rang and David opened his door to find Homer standing in the hallway—alone.

"She's here," Homer assured him. "She's in the car with Rose. I wanted a minute alone with you first."

"That's probably smart," David agreed. "What do I need to know?"

"Only that there isn't a lot for me to tell you," Homer explained, removing his pipe from between his lips. "As you know, she suffered another attack. She lost consciousness for a while, and when she came to she had symptoms of a stroke. She should recover her mental faculties in time, but whether she'll ever be a hundred percent again remains to be seen. Her heart seems to be doing well." He paused and relit his pipe. "She's responding to the medicine nicely, and her blood pressure is normal. Now what she needs more than anything is rest."

"I'll make sure she stays put," David said grimly. His green eyes flashed with determination. "I don't want to risk her having another heart attack."

"Exactly right." Homer nodded in approval and pointed his pipe at David. "Which leads me to a very important warning. Until her heart has had a chance to mend, don't let her get excited over anything. Keep her quiet and calm. Stay agreeable, no matter how confused she seems."

"I'm pretty sure I can do that much. Is she still pretty mixed up?" David jangled the keys in his pocket nervously.

"Yes. For example, she's been calling me Bertie, and I haven't corrected her. Her doctor agrees with me. We feel the shock wouldn't be good for her at this point."

The elevator bell chimed, and when the doors slid open, Rose helped Abigail out, half supporting and half carrying her down the hallway.

"Bertie?" Abigail's tiny voice called. "Bertie, are you there?"

"Right here, Abby," Homer answered. Looking over his shoulder at David, he whispered, "See what I mean?"

David nodded and followed all three of them into his home. He was relieved to see that Abigail looked much better than he'd expected. She was wearing her favorite traveling suit, a soft, pink wool with a ruffled white blouse. At her throat rested a large ivory cameo, and an ornate ivory comb drew her long gray hair into a bun on top of her head. Two high spots of color stained her cheeks, and her eyes were alert.

They settled her on the sofa and then stood back anxiously, wondering how she would adapt.

"Abigail, you remember your grandson David?" Homer spoke slowly."

"Well, of course I remember him!" Abigail snapped. "Bertie, do stop treating me like I've lost my mind. David, come sit with me." She beckoned to him and patted the cushion beside her on the sofa.

David sat down in the seat next to her and reached over to take one of her frail hands in his strong one. "How are you doing, Gran?" he asked her gently.

"I'm just fine," she said with a sniff. Then she lowered her voice. "But just try telling that to your grandfather and his fussbudget friend."

Rose snorted at that. "Abigail, are you ready for your visit with David?" She came around and wedged herself in between David and the arm of the sofa.

Abigail nodded happily. "My, yes. David, how long has it been since I visited you and your family?"

David was nonplussed for a moment. *Good grief.* She must know that she was his only family. She couldn't be thinking his folks were still alive, could she? "I—I don't know," he stammered.

Rose nudged him with her round elbow and sent him a "didn't I tell you?" look. His eyes pleaded with Homer for help.

"I believe it was sometime last year, before David moved." Homer offered. They all stared at Abigail to see how she would react.

Clearly puzzled, she nodded slowly. "That's probably true." She brightened. "I'm sure looking forward to spending some time with you all."

All who? All what? David wondered. *My law books? My furniture? My clients?* "Yes," he answered, because he didn't know what else to say.

Rose slapped her thighs, and the sound reverberated throughout the room. "We'd probably better unload the car and be on our way. I've got a plane to catch." She accepted Homer's labored assistance in getting up off the sofa.

The two men stowed Abigail's half-dozen suitcases and assorted cartons in the spare bedroom. David was astonished at the amount of stuff she was bringing with her. Just how long was it going to take to recover from this thing? She had enough gear to last a year. When they were finished, David, Homer and Rose met in the hallway to say goodbye.

"Thank you, honey." Rose squeezed David's arm tightly. "You don't know what this means to me. Did Homer tell you about her medicine?" At Homer's negative grunt, she continued. "Her medicine is in her suitcase. She gets four pills a day. Three with meals, and one before bedtime. I have written down my daughter's phone number in Arizona, and Abigail's doctor's name and phone number, in case of an emergency. It's in with her pills. You shouldn't need it, but you never know."

"That's right," Homer chimed in. "And she's got a doctor's appointment next Thursday. Weather permitting, I'll come down and get her for that. You'll need a break by then, my boy. Caring for the sick can be taxing."

I'll say, David thought to himself. She'd just arrived, and already he felt exhausted. And worried. What if something went wrong? He was beginning to have second thoughts. Maybe Abigail needed more help than he could give. Professional help. Doctors. Nurses. An operating room, for crying out loud.

"Call me if you run into any problems," Homer said.

David glanced into the living room at Abigail. Her gray bun was barely visible over the top of the sofa. The poignant picture was overwhelming. A lump formed in his throat. He felt incredibly protective toward this tiny woman who had always been larger-than-life.

"I will, Homer," David promised. "I guess I'll see you Thursday?"

"Yes." Homer looked a little lost. "Take care of her, David. She's a special lady."

"Will do, sir." David shook his hand. "Rose, Merry Christmas, if I don't see you sooner. And remember, other people will want to hold that baby, too," he teased.

"I will, honey." Rose kissed his cheek. "Thanks again."

Smiling, David shut the door, anxiety gnawing at his stomach. What would he talk about with Abigail, now that Rose and Homer were gone? He needn't have worried. The tiny woman on the sofa was already fast asleep.

Lauren slept in late on Saturday morning. When she finally glanced at the clock, it was already ten. Pushing Hairball off her neck, she sat up and looked at the press photo of herself on the nightstand. She leaned over and pulled a pad of paper and a pen out of a drawer.

So, David's grandmother wanted an autograph today, hmmm? For the life of her, she couldn't think of a single clever thing to write. Doodling on the pad for a moment, she experimented with several ideas, but nothing seemed right.

Oh, this is ridiculous, Lauren thought. It shouldn't be this hard. In her best handwriting, she carefully signed her name, while the cat chased her pen. Blowing on the damp ink, she inspected the finished product. The black-and-white glossy was very glamorous. It was one of the best pictures she'd ever had taken, and a delicious thrill swirled in her stomach at the thought of David seeing it. Today was the day. Come hell or high water, she was going to ask the buckaroo across the hall to the dance. She tossed the pad and photo down on the nightstand, jumped out of bed and ran to the bathroom to get ready.

David was just getting Abigail settled in the guest bedroom when the doorbell rang.

"I'll go see who that is, Gran." He finished plumping up her pillow and tucked it behind her back. "Stay in bed and get some rest, okay? I don't want you up running around," he said with a mock frown.

"Don't mind me, now. You go along." She smiled up at him from under the thick comforter.

David went into the living room and pulled his front door open to find Lauren standing there smiling and holding a manila envelope. Even though he'd expected her to drop in sometime that day, he was not prepared for the tropical storm that thundered through him at the sight of her.

Her long hair was swept up in a loose ponytail. Stray wisps of hair had fallen out of the clasp and lay casually around her face. She wore an old gray sweatshirt pushed up at the elbows, faded blue jeans, and running shoes. She was stunning.

"Lauren!" Her name escaped unconsciously. "Come on in," he said, recovering.

"Lauren?" Abigail cried from the bedroom.

They both turned and glanced at the open door.

"I'm not interrupting anything, am I?" she asked uncertainly.

"Don't be silly. I'm glad you're here." His eyes drank her in, as he took the envelope out of her hand.

"Lauren? Is that you, honey?" Abigail called again.

David looked over his shoulder at the guest room again. "My grandmother must have heard us talking," he explained. "She probably wants to meet you."

Lauren smiled. "I'd love to meet her, too."

Setting her picture on his coffee table, he took her hand and led her to Abigail's room. *What on earth was it about his incredible hands?* she wondered. One touch and her senses were spinning.

"Gran." David pulled Lauren out from behind him. "Gran, this is Lauren."

Abigail Barclay drew herself up on the pillows and sighed in exasperation.

"David, of course I know Lauren. After all, she *is* your wife."

Chapter Four

Lauren and David looked at each other, then at Abigail, then at each other again. Lauren cleared her throat as if to speak, but no words came out. Sensing what she was about to do, David jumped in.

"Uh . . . sweetheart, do I smell something burning?" He put his arm around Lauren's shoulder and motioned her out the door with his head.

"What?" She stared at him quizzically. Had he gone mad? Had the old woman? She wasn't his wife or his sweetheart, and she was going to set both of these lunatics straight, right now.

"No. No, I don't smell anything burning. I smell a rat. I'd like to know just what the—"

"The smell is?" he finished for her, still motioning her out of the room with his head. "No, I don't think it's a rat, dear. We got rid of those last week, remember?"

"Oh, my goodness, I hope so! I do hate rats," Abigail said in alarm.

"Don't worry, Gran." He grabbed Lauren's wrist. "I think it's probably the...soup we're fixing for you, burning or something."

"Well, go see about it, David. I don't like fire, either," Abigail fretted.

"Not to worry, Gran, I'm sure it's nothing." David yanked Lauren tightly to his side. "We'll put it out. You just try and stay calm."

"Now wait just a darn minute!" Lauren sputtered.

"We don't have a minute, darling." He practically dragged her out of the room behind him.

"Let go of me!" Lauren snapped when they had reached the living room. "What on earth is going on? What fire? Where? And why did you tell your grandmother we're married?" She regarded him warily.

David dropped Lauren's arm, and rubbed his temples tiredly. "I didn't tell her we're married. Honest. And there is no fire. Sorry, I panicked. I just didn't know what else to do." His voice was hushed. "Come into the kitchen with me while I make her some soup, and I'll do my best to explain."

Lauren followed him into the kitchen, glancing around curiously as she went. His condo was exactly like hers, only backward. And where hers was tidy and designer-perfect, his was masculine, and in need of a woman's touch. Kind of like him, she reflected.

She liked his home. It was bold and stark, but comfortable and lived-in. The musky smell reminded her of spicy after-shave, and clean, strong male. She felt safe, protected and very much at home here. She gave herself a mental shake. *Whoa, girl.* Get ahold of yourself. Of course you feel at home here. Your place is exactly like his.

Pots and pans rattled as he hunched over and searched through his disorganized cabinets. "Damn." He rocked back on his heels, resting his arms on his thighs.

"What's wrong?" she came around the counter and looked down at him.

"I can't find my microwave bowl." He grinned up at her apologetically.

"Okay. I'll make the soup, and you tell me about our *marriage*," she said, and began methodically poking her head into his cupboards.

David winced at her sarcasm. Standing up, he leaned back against the counter, crossed his ankles and folded his arms over his broad chest.

"Okay. Gran is staying with me while she recuperates from another mild heart attack. Something happened when she had this attack. I don't really understand everything, but somehow it affected her mind. She's confused. She thinks her neighbor is my grandfather, stuff like that."

"Sounds like a stroke." Lauren found the can opener and used it on a can of alphabet soup.

"Sort of, I guess. Anyway, her doctor says her heart can't take any kind of shock. That's why Homer—that's her neighbor—hasn't told her that my grandfather is dead. The shock might be too much for her."

Lauren emptied the contents of the can into a small pot and turned a burner on to medium. "Oh, no, that's terrible. Shouldn't she be in a hospital or something?"

"That's what I thought, but they say physically she's improving, and mentally she should snap out of it, given time."

"So, this is why she thinks we're married?"

"Probably. She watches you on TV all the time, and she's been harping on me getting married for years. She just can't seem to accept the fact that I'm happy without a wife. Happier by far than most of my clients. I guess her mixed-up mind must have put all the pieces together backward."

So, he wasn't married. Turning to reach for a spoon, Lauren nearly walked into David. She hadn't heard him come up behind her. He was so close she could feel the warmth radiating off his body. The white T-shirt he wore was stretched tight across his chest and stomach. She had the absurd impulse to reach up and run her hands over the gentle hills and valleys of his powerful build.

Looking up into his dark emerald eyes, she asked, "What should we do?" Her voice quavered.

He lounged casually against the edge of the stove and pondered her question. He knew what he'd like to do.

"I don't know." He took the spoon out of her hand and stirred the soup.

"Well, we don't want to upset her. She could have another heart attack or stroke or whatever." Lauren's eyes, wide with worry, regarded him seriously.

"That's what scares me." He pulled a tray out of an overhead cabinet and set it on the counter. "Lately she's been talking a lot about what's going to happen to me after she's gone. She's the only family I've got, and she worries about me being all alone in the world and all."

"Mmm..." Lauren nodded sympathetically.

"Since her heart's been giving her trouble, she's really been on the marriage bandwagon."

"Let me see if I have this straight." Lauren pinched the bridge of her nose and shut her eyes tight. "You can't just go in there and tell her you're not married. It would kill her. Is that right?"

"Yes, but I don't know what else to do." His voice reflected his frustration. "She's going to figure it out when you're not here."

Lauren thought for a moment as she picked up the spoon and tasted the soup. They had a problem. She turned the heat down under the soup and got a bowl out of his cupboard.

"You said something about her snapping out of this...'condition.' What did you mean?"

David lifted the pot off the burner, reached past Lauren and filled the bowl with soup. His body smoldered where he'd brushed against her. He cleared his throat. "Homer says that most people come out of these kinds of things in a few weeks. Sometimes longer, but they almost always get better."

"How does Homer know?" she asked skeptically.

"He's a doctor. Dr. Homer Penwalt."

"Oh. Then he would know." Searching around in the re-frigerator, Lauren found a bottle of orange juice, poured a glass for Abigail and set it on the tray. Soda crackers, a napkin, silverware and condiments followed. Frowning, she pulled the salt off the tray and put it back in the spice cup-board. "Blood pressure," she explained. "She needs all the help she can get to . . . snap out of it," she finished lamely.

"Lauren." He sighed. "I'm going to be straight with you." He took her by the shoulders and slowly turned her around to face him. "I don't like this any better than you do. But the way I see it, we don't have much choice."

"I'm not sure I know what you mean." Lauren picked up Abigail's tray in an effort to put some space between her and this compelling man.

"I mean we play along with her."

Lauren set the tray back down. "You *are* kidding?"

"Just until she eats her soup. Then she'll probably sleep. And then, well, maybe she'll forget."

"What if she doesn't? That won't work. Why don't we just tell her we're getting a divorce?"

"No." He placed his hands belligerently on his narrow hips.

"What do you mean, no?"

"Oh, come on, Lauren, a divorce would be even worse. You should hear how she preaches about my sleazeball cli-ents. I don't want her keeling over on the spot."

"Do you have any better ideas?" She folded her arms across her breasts.

That simple movement sent a herd of butterflies stam-peding through his stomach. Buffalo-sized butterflies. "Yes." He looked up at her face. "I mean, no."

"So?"

"Look, you're an actress. So act. This kind of thing should come easily to you."

His encouraging tone made her flush with shame. Guilt-ily she bit her lip and looked away. Oh, great. Now that damn lie about the play was coming back to haunt her. Served her right. She was getting herself in deep. First she

lied to him about being in some rodeo version of *Our Town,*
and now more lies to keep Grandma alive. She hated liars.
How had she gotten into this mess? And to think all she had
ever wanted out of him was a date for the mayor's Christmas ball. A light bulb went on in Lauren's head. The time
to round 'em up was now.

She smiled tentatively. "I'll make a deal with you."

David lifted a questioning eyebrow. "What kind of
deal?"

She drew a deep breath. "You've heard of the mayor's
Christmas ball?" When he nodded, she hurried on. "For
reasons I don't care to discuss...I need an escort." Her jaw
tensed. "So, here's the deal. I play along with your little
game till Grandma goes to sleep, and you help me out with
the ball."

"Deal," he said, and held out his hand. Was he dreaming? This was too good to be true. She'd agreed to help him,
she'd asked him out on a date, and, best of all she was
shaking hands with him. No, she wasn't just shaking his
hand, she was setting him on fire. Fire. That reminded him.

"We'd better go back in there. She's waiting."

"Okay then. We're married, but just until she goes to
sleep." Lauren wanted to make it clear she was complying
unwillingly. "This is against my better judgment. What if we
really screw it up?"

"Right now, shocking her with news that we're not married would really screw it up. What have we got to lose?"

"*My* mind, for starters. But I guess you're right." She
picked up the tray again. "David? About the acting thing?"
She saw his worried expression and changed her mind. "I'll
tell you later. Just follow my lead."

He squeezed her arm gently and led her back to Abigail's
room. "Thanks, I owe you one."

"Hope you can dance," she muttered.

Abigail was still sitting up in bed when they got back to
her room.

"How's the fire?" she asked, looking back and forth between the two of them.

"Oh, just fine, um....Gran." Lauren swooped over to the bed and set the tray down on the older woman's lap. "I had, uh, forgotten about the soup."

"That's right. The soup. Lauren is still learning the fine art of being the perfect wife, aren't you, sweetheart?" David's eyes twinkled at her.

She sent him a quelling stare. "Yes, it will be a while before I master alphabet soup."

Abigail reached over and patted her hand. "Don't worry, honey. When I was first married, I couldn't boil water. You'll learn." She smiled and began eating her soup, reminiscing about the many wifely duties Lauren apparently had yet to learn. "I think cooking and cleaning are perhaps two of the most important keys to success in a marriage. Today, those fine arts are shoved aside in favor of meaningless careers for women. No time to learn to cook. Oh, no..." Gran tsked.

Lauren rolled her eyes in disbelief.

"Oh, don't worry, Gran, she's learning," David agreed gleefully. "She's a very talented woman. I'm sure she does *many* things quite well."

Lauren's face went pink. "Shut up," she groused under her breath. He was having altogether too much fun.

She deliberately changed the subject. "How's the soup...er...Gran?"

Abigail pushed the half-empty bowl of soup back on her tray. "It was delicious, darling. The best I've ever had."

Lauren looked at the little woman's sunny face and felt a sudden surge of affection for her. She could see why David wanted to protect her so badly. She looked over at him with a new understanding. He really was a sweet man.

Picking the tray up off the bed, she said, "I'm glad."

Abigail smiled at her tiredly. "I'm afraid your wonderful lunch has made me quite sleepy. So, if you two lovebirds will excuse me..." Settling back onto the pillows, she shooed them out of the room.

David followed Lauren back into his kitchen. He had to give her credit—she'd been a real sport about the whole mess. Or maybe not...

Lauren whirled to face him, her blue eyes shooting sparks of anger. "Just what did you think you were doing in there?" she demanded. "I agreed to play along with *her*. Not to lead her to believe there was some undying love between us, let alone that I was your maid!"

"I guess I got carried away in the heat of the moment." He looked faintly amused.

"I'll say you did, *sweetheart*." Lauren began unloading the tray. "You've probably done irreparable damage," she said accusingly. "Next she'll be wondering where David Junior is."

"We could dress Hairball in baby pajamas," he offered.

Lauren had to bite the inside of her cheek to keep from laughing. "This is not funny," she stated. Then she laughed in spite of herself. "Do you think she'd buy it?"

"The way things have been going, nothing would surprise me." He joined her in a stress-relieving belly laugh. Their laughter was contagious, and soon they were both gasping for air. When the laughter had died down, they stood there, just looking at each other.

She was so beautiful when she laughed. David felt a restless arousal in the pit of his stomach. Slowly he reached out and drew her to him. He hugged her gently for a moment. "Thank you for helping me out in there." He tilted her head back and studied her face. "You're a good sport."

Lauren stood in the circle of his arms, tongue-tied. Her heart pounded thunderously in her ears. Shaking his hand was nothing compared to the thrill she felt as he caressed her lower back. She'd never felt this way in Joe's arms. Pleasant and warm, yes, but nothing like this.

Feeling the need for some distance, she took a small step backward. Regret flashed briefly in his eyes as he released her.

Lauren walked over to the kitchen window and peered out. "Looks like snow," she commented.

"Really?" He came and stood directly behind her. He surveyed the view over her shoulder. Snow-laden clouds were filling the sky and blocking out the sun. Naked trees stood like lonely soldiers against the darkening horizon. She shivered and wondered if it was because of the weather or the man.

"I'm glad I don't have to drive to work this week." Her voice sounded unsteady in her ears.

"Why not?" His breath tickled the back of her neck.

"I'm on vacation for a couple of weeks. I had some time to use up before I lost it," she explained.

"That's great." He was elated. "For you, I mean. Do you have plans?"

"No. I'm just taking it easy." Now that she and Joe weren't going to the Bahamas, taking it easy was her only option.

"Mmm..." He turned and walked over to the counter, and she felt an unexplainable chill. "I'll be home, too. I'm going to try working out of the house while Gran is here."

"Ah." Lauren turned and leaned against the window. "I suppose I'd better be going."

Maybe it was his imagination, but the room seemed to grow suddenly darker with her words. "Thanks again...for everything." He lifted and then dropped his hands. "You really bailed me out on this one."

"No problem." She smiled. "If you need anything for..."

"Abigail," he supplied.

"Abigail." She repeated the name. "Just put your lips together and...blow." She grinned. "It doesn't look like I'm going anywhere."

"I think I can take it from here." He smiled back at her wryly. They walked to the front door together, neither of them speaking.

She hesitated in the hallway. "Let me know how she's doing." She looked over his shoulder toward the guest room.

"I will, and thanks again."

* * *

Lauren spent the afternoon cleaning out her hall closet. She was up to her ears in tennis rackets and ski gear when the phone rang. David? Stumbling over a pile of games and coats, she grabbed the phone by the cord and pulled it off the coffee table. Polly's voice droned into the room through the headset as she dragged the phone over her mountain of paraphernalia.

"I'm here!" she yelled. "Don't hang up!" Gasping, she stretched out prone on the floor to reach the receiver. "Hello?" she panted.

"Either you've just been shoveling snow, or I've interrupted something juicy," Polly said.

"Neither. I'm cleaning out my hall closet." Lauren turned over on her back and propped her feet up on an old box of videotapes.

"Wow. You really know how to throw a vacation." Polly snored loudly.

"A lot you know. I've had an interesting morning."

"Oh, yeah? What'd ya do? Clean and polish your silver for laughs?"

"No. I got married." Lauren held the phone away from her ear to avoid Polly's ear-piercing screech.

"You *what?* Without me? So, I really am interrupting your honeymoon?" she cried.

"No. It's not a real marriage. It was just pretend."

"Damn." Polly's voice deflated like a punctured tire. "I'm waiting. What's the deal?"

"Remember my neighbor across the hall?"

"Tall, dark and gorgeous hunk of throbbing manliness?"

"The same. Remember I told you about his grandmother being sick?"

"Yes," Polly answered.

"She's had a heart attack, and it affected her memory. She's not mental or anything, just confused, so she's staying with him while she recuperates."

"I've heard about that. The same thing happened to my mom's uncle Fred. Poor guy. For weeks he thought he was Frank Sinatra. Drove us all crazy. The man cannot sing."

"Luckily, she's not that bad," Lauren giggled. "She just thinks I'm David's wife."

"No kidding? Cool!" Polly cooed jealously.

"Are you nuts? This is a nightmare. I only agreed to play along with it for the afternoon in exchange for a date for the ball. I hope she's already snapped out of it. One false move and it's curtains. Her doctor says a sudden shock could really hurt her."

"Sorry," Polly said. "But, hey! You've got a date to the ball. And after that, who knows? This might be the perfect opportunity to get up close and personal with Mr. Wonderful."

"No way. I just got out of a relationship. I don't want another one. I'm a busy woman. No, a simple date to the ball will suffice."

"Right." Polly's voice dripped with sarcasm. "Well, get back to your closet. I've got glitter balls to glue."

"Look who's talking, Miss Life-styles of the Arts and Crafts. What's a glitter ball?"

"Styrofoam ball ornaments with the kid's names written in glitter. I'm thinking of changing my name to Peggy. That way I don't have to fix the drips."

"Okay, Peggy, I'll talk to you later."

"You bet you will. Darn." The phone beeped in Lauren's ear. "I think I just glued my hand to the phone. Shoot. Call me later."

That evening David picked up the phone and squinted at the scrap of paper Rose had tucked in with Abigail's pills. There appeared to be two phone numbers written there, but he'd be darned if he could decipher them. Was that a seven or a one? A three or a five? A nine or a four? This was ridiculous. He couldn't call everyone in Sea Grove looking for Abigail's doctor. Directory assistance could probably help, if he could read the doctor's name. It looked like Dr. Argentine. Or Augustine. Or Anaheim. With his luck, he'd end up talking to Disneyland. Disgusted, he crumpled the paper and threw it on the coffee table. He dialed Homer instead.

Homer confirmed David's suspicion that having Lauren play along with Abigail's confusion over his marital status had been the right thing to do.

David was so frustrated, he felt like wringing Lauren's pretty little neck. If it weren't for her, Gran wouldn't think he was married, and he wouldn't be in this jam.

To make matters worse, Homer was afraid that if they confessed the truth to Abigail at this delicate stage in her recovery the shock could prove fatal.

"I could call Lauren and explain the dangers," Homer offered.

No, this was his mess, and he'd handle it. "Thanks anyway, Homer," he said decisively. "I'll take care of it."

He hung up the phone and rubbed his tired eyes. Too much stress. He was beginning to feel like a jailbird. If it weren't for this stupid snow, he could go running. He could run away and never come back. But that wasn't his style. David never ran away from his problems. He faced them head-on. And that was what he'd do now. Face his problem head on.

Okay. So facing Abigail head-on was out of the question. But he could face Lauren head-on. The very thought tired him out. It was at times like this that marriage didn't sound so bad. At least he'd have someone to rub his aching back. The feel of holding Lauren in his arms came flooding into his mind. She was so soft and feminine. And she smelled good. When she'd tilted her head back and looked up at him all nervous and sexy like that, it had taken all his willpower not to kiss her senseless. No. He couldn't do that. He needed her help with Abigail. It wouldn't do to come across like some kind of caveman. He wondered what she was doing now. Probably sleeping like a baby.

* * *

Lauren was pacing around the Oriental rug on her living room floor. Hairball, curled up in the wingback chair, followed her movements with one open eye.

"No news is good news, Hairy. She must have figured out we're not really married. Maybe she's even forgotten who I am."

"Meah." Hairball yawned.

"You really think so?" She stopped in front of his chair and scratched his ears. Lauren wondered if ten o'clock at night was too late to call and find out how Abigail was doing. Oh, well, it didn't matter. She didn't know David's phone number anyway.

Not feeling a bit sleepy, she wandered over to the hall closet, where a pile of Christmas decorations still sat on the floor. Dragging a box of tree lights into the living room, she slowly and carefully began to untangle them. Only fifteen shopping days till Christmas, she counted. At least this year she didn't need to include Joe on her who's-been-nice list. He was definitely at the top of her naughty list, to put it mildly.

Tanya would be shopping for his gift this year. She'd probably just tie a bow around her neck and give herself to him, Lauren thought spitefully. Unconsciously she tied the strand of lights she was working on into a bow and tightened it with a convulsive yank. A bulb snapped, and she stared at the broken glass. It was clear she still hadn't dealt with all the emotional fallout from her breakup with Joe.

Time for a mental pep talk, she decided, picking up the sharp pieces of glass and tossing them in the garbage. She knew she was a very fortunate woman. She had good health, she had an education, she had a loving family, she had a career she loved, she had friends, she had Hairball.

Tanya had Joe. Big deal. She had... Well, she didn't need a man she told herself sternly. No time for romantic involvement. Except for an occasional escort, she amended. So why did she feel so lost?

She was beginning to realize that even though she hadn't been passionately in love with Joe, she'd needed him more than she was willing to admit. He'd kept her from examining her need for a committed relationship. Funny how life throws you a curveball when you least expect it, she thought wryly. She'd somehow allowed herself to think that nothing would ever change. She'd had her work, and Joe's occasional companionship, and she'd been complete. *Had been.*

Her career had become her whole life. So much so that she didn't even know what to do with herself when she had time off. Even though she'd tried to see the bright side of not traveling with Joe, what had seemed like a dream vacation of loafing around and recharging now yawned drearily in front of her. Fifteen shopping days.

Lauren finished untwining the last string of lights and coiled it neatly in the box with the others. Better get a tree pretty soon, she thought. That would be something to do. The clock on the wall chimed 10:30. Maybe a hot bath would put her to sleep.

Piling her hair on the top of her head, she filled the Jacuzzi in her master bath with water and bubble bath. She slipped beneath the blanket of hot, foamy suds and willed herself to relax. A feeling of melancholy settled over her, and, try as she might, she couldn't pinpoint why. She didn't really miss Joe. In fact, he hadn't crossed her mind that much all week. Although the thought of him skipping happily off into the sunset with Tanya did grate on her nerves. He was living it up, while she had nothing exciting to look forward to.

It was then that it dawned on her. She was bored. Bored stiff. Time for a plan of action. That was what she needed. Action. Now all she had to do was think of the action. Frowning, she explored the faucet with her toe.

The clock on her living room wall chimed the hour. Eight, nine, ten, she thought, counting. Eleven, twelve, thirteen.

Thirteen o'clock? That couldn't be right. She must have miscounted. No, there it was again. *Bing, bong. Bing, bong.*

That wasn't her clock. That was her doorbell. Who would be ringing her doorbell at this hour? Fear of the unknown gave her goose bumps as she reached for her silk bathrobe.

David was beginning to lose his nerve. What if she was in bed already? He jammed his hands in his jeans pockets and tried to peer through the peephole in Lauren's door. Couldn't see a thing.

On the other side of the door, Lauren looked through her peephole to see one huge green eye staring back at her. She gasped and tightened her revealing robe around her body.

"Who's there?" she called nervously.

"It's me. David, from across the hall." He took a step back and suddenly came into focus. Smiling tentatively, he looked vulnerable and boyish. Her thoughts sprang to Abigail. It must be an emergency. Filled with panic, she fumbled with the locks on her door.

"Hang on just a minute," she squeaked, making a grab for the damp robe with her free hand. Top to the right, middle to the left, bottom to the right.

"Damn!" she muttered as she tried to open the door. Still locked. Frantically she clutched her gaping robe closed. Whoever installed these deadbolt locks should be shot. *Sorry, Daddy,* she thought. Okay. Top to the left. Still locked. "Damn, damn. Hang on, I'm coming."

David's smile grew wider.

She was glad the place wasn't on fire. She'd be burned to a crisp by now. Bottom to the left. In frustration, she yanked on the door as hard as she could, and it flew open with a force that knocked her backward.

David jumped in and caught her just before she fell all the way to the ground. Unfortunately, due to her hasty exit from the tub, her silk robe was damp and slippery. Slithering out of David's grasp, she fell down, in a most unladylike fashion, pulling him neatly on top of her.

"Ouch!" she yelped.

Stunned, David looked down at the woman who had so thoughtfully cushioned his landing. His eyes widened in shock as he took in the damp robe, molded with little subtlety to her perfect body.

"Get off me!" Lauren grunted as she grabbed for the sash of her robe with one hand and pushed at the firm chest that hovered over her with the other.

David's eyes shot to her face and saw the crimson heat stealing into her cheeks. "I'm so sorry! I was just trying to—" he pulled the lapel of her robe up and wrapped it over Lauren's breasts, tucking it under her chin "—help," he finished awkwardly, averting his eyes. His hand was still planted firmly on her middle, and Lauren could feel her flesh burning from his touch.

"Would you mind?" she gasped, struggling to disentangle her legs gracefully from his.

Sitting up, he lifted his bottom and pulled the hem of the silky robe out from under him. Eyes still averted, he struggled to cover her long, shapely legs. Flesh. Warm, soft, slightly damp feminine flesh. David's hand froze. His heart was hammering raw desire throughout his body, and his breathing was ragged.

"David." Lauren's voice was surprisingly calm. "Please. I can handle it from here."

David jerked his hand away as if he'd been slapped. "Sorry," he stammered, "I was just—"

"Trying to help. I know." Lauren's voice held an amused note.

He turned and looked at the woman who was now sitting next to him, modestly covered by her robe. Her cheeks were still rosy from her bath, and her hair fell like spun silk in wild disarray around her shoulders. He had never wanted anyone as badly as he wanted her at that moment.

David was by no means inexperienced when it came to women. He'd casually dated more women than he'd care to remember. Heck, he'd had girls chasing him since the second grade, when Lucy Cartwright had beaten the crap out of him because she liked him. But none of these women had ever compelled him the way Lauren Wills did.

Something about her drew him inexplicably into the depths of her dark blue eyes. Slowly he reached up and stroked her flushed cheek with the back of his hand. Seductively his gaze slid downward, lingering hungrily on her curves. She shivered involuntarily, and he dropped his hand.

Their eyes met and locked. The look she saw there sent a rush of new feelings coursing through her. For the first time in her life, Lauren knew what it felt like to be overwhelmingly attracted to a man. Something about the raw power in his touch sent her heart leaping with exhilaration.

She felt utterly feminine when she was with him, and the idea that he was attracted to her excited her unbelievably. She was trembling, and her teeth were beginning to chatter. David reached over and kicked her front door shut with the heel of his boot.

"You're cold," he stated matter-of-factly.

"Mmm, hmm..." She nodded.

Standing up, he reached down and pulled Lauren to her feet and into his arms. He rubbed his hands briskly over her back in an effort to warm her up. His hands stilled for a moment.

"You're beautiful," he whispered, and she knew he was referring to what he'd seen earlier. She colored again.

"Don't," he murmured, stroking her heated cheek. "Trust me—you don't have anything to be embarrassed about. You're—" he closed the distance between their faces "—breathtaking."

It was supposed to be a closed-mouthed, platonic kiss. The kind exchanged by two people who were just being neighborly. A little peck to reassure Lauren that what had just happened had no effect on him whatsoever. Wrong. The problem was, once David's lips touched hers, he knew he had to have more or die.

Heart pounding, Lauren felt a sudden, incredible urge to get a taste of something new and thrilling that she'd obviously been missing out on with Joe. Leaning forward on her toes, she pressed her mouth more firmly into his soft, sexy lips and boldly tasted him with her tongue. The room was silent, except for the thrumming of her heart and the heavy, greedy breathing of her neighbor.

Her neighbor! Good Lord! What was she doing? She barely knew this guy! And here she was, standing half-naked, getting acquainted with the dark recesses of his mouth. Had she lost her mind?

Gasping, she broke away from him and leaned against the wall for support. He seemed equally shaken and confused.

"I—I'd better go get dressed," she stammered and suddenly remembered that she didn't know why he was here. "Is everything okay?" she asked.

"Perfect," he breathed.

"I mean with your grandmother." The corner of her mouth lifted slightly, but then she frowned. "Is anything wrong?"

"Oh." He smiled lazily at her. "That's what I came to talk to you about. Go get dressed, and we'll talk." He turned Lauren around and reluctantly pushed her toward the bedroom.

Lauren hastily ran a brush through her hair and lightly applied some quick makeup. She snapped the top of her lipstick tube back in place and surveyed her reflection in the mirror. Her eyes sparkled back at her, and she fairly beamed with excitement. Frowning, she pulled on an oversized hot-pink sweatshirt.

What had happened to her stern resolve to stay away from men? They were nothing but trouble and heartache, yet here she was acting like a breathless schoolgirl. *I'm fickle,* she thought in horror. For someone who prided herself on not being shallow, she sure wasn't pining away after Joe. Or maybe she was. Maybe she was on the rebound. Oh, no... This was awful. She was playing the fool again. Angrily, she jerked her light pink leggings up and stuffed her feet into a pair of slouch socks. How could I be such a boob? A guy dumps me and I go and get all mushy over the boy next door. Embarrassed, she thought about how she had just responded to David.

She'd always been the type of person who was in control. No one ever caught her wearing her heart on her sleeve. Until now. Something about this man turned her into a quivering mass of lusting Jell-O. Well, not anymore.

Lauren took a deep breath. It wasn't too late, she resolved, to gain the upper hand in this matter. Nonchalant. Yes. That was it. She had to act nonchalant. Friendly, yet cool. Determined to set the record straight, Lauren strode into the living room.

David was sitting on her couch, vigorously rubbing Hairball's well-rounded stomach. Lounging in David's lap, the cat looked as if he'd died and gone to kitty heaven. His eyes were squeezed tightly shut, and his cheeks were puffed up in what she could have sworn was a smile.

David's eyes followed her appreciatively as she walked over and sat down in her wingback chair.

"What can I do for you?" she asked in her most professional tone.

David set the cat on the floor and leaned forward. "Well, actually, I came over to ask you to marry me."

Chapter Five

"The fact of the matter is, I'm not asking you, I'm begging you."

Lauren was completely and totally nonplussed.

"Just for the next few days or so." He watched her closely, trying to gauge her reaction. When there was none, he forged ahead. "I don't know what else to do. When she woke up from her nap, she wanted to know where you were. I pleaded a headache for you, to buy some time. I called her friend, Homer, and he thinks we did the right thing this morning by going along with her. Homer said that if we don't play along with her little head trip, anything could happen." David's eyes glittered with danger and purpose.

"And I *will not* let any harm come to that woman. I'd move heaven and earth for her, fight armies, slay dragons. Don't make me start with you. So, bottom line—are you with me or not?" he asked her boldly.

Lauren was still reeling. Not helping David at this point seemed unnecessarily cruel. Especially in light of the fact that she had nothing to do, and couldn't have gone anywhere even if she had. But, on the other hand, becoming entangled in his problem was something she did *not* relish. Lauren struggled for a moment with an inner battle. She couldn't let a sweet old lady die, just because she was fed up with the male population. But if she was going to help, there would have to be ground rules. He was going to owe her big on this Christmas ball thing. Visions of flowers and limousines danced through her head. The silence between them was deafening.

"Well?" David demanded. His patience was wearing thin.

"What about Hairball?" She knew she was grasping at straws.

"Damn it! I don't care! Bring him along. Gran always wanted great-grandchildren," he said in agitation. "We can start tomorrow, with Sunday brunch or whatever. You'll need to be there before she wakes up." He was planning already.

"Hey, wait a minute. I haven't agreed yet."

"Oh, come on, Lauren!" he nearly shouted. "What's it to you? It's snowing too deep to go anywhere. What else are you going to do?"

"I have plans!" she said, raising her voice defensively.

"What? To lie around all week?" he asked with derision.

"No!"

"Then what? Tell me what's more important than a human life!"

He had her there. Suddenly her petty anger at Joe seemed insignificant. Still, she was afraid. Afraid they might make a very harmful mistake with Abigail. Afraid of her attraction to this man. Afraid of losing control.

"What if something goes wrong? What if I mess up and she goes into some kind of attack?"

"Don't worry. You won't mess up. You're not the type."

"Don't patronize me."

"I'm not! You're smart. You'll be fine. Besides, I'll be there."

Lauren looked at David and was immersed in his power-ful self-confidence. All her earlier resolve to remain distant from him melted into so many puddles of nothing. He was a very single-minded man. How could she fight his logic? Besides, this was a plan of action. Maybe not the action she had figured on, but at least she wouldn't be bored.

"You're really in a bind, aren't you?" At his nod, she sighed in resignation. "Okay, I'll help you."

Relief smoothed the lines of David's face. "You will? Hallelujah! Look, I know this isn't what you planned to do with your time off, but somehow I'll make it up to you. I promise."

"I said I'd help you, but I want to make a few things clear before I do."

"Shoot."

"For one thing, we need to plan our strategy. You know, get our story straight. I don't want some dumb slip of the tongue to send her over the edge. If we're going to do it, let's do it right."

"Great. What else?"

"I'm staying here at night. During the day we're . . . well, married. When she's asleep, I'm off duty."

"Awww . . ." He grinned at her.

"If I'd wanted a husband, I'd be married by now. I just ended one relationship, and I have no desire to start an-other."

David might have looked crestfallen, but underneath he was thrilled. No boyfriend!

"I mean it! No funny business," she said.

"None?" He raised his eyebrows innocently.

"Only enough to convince her that we're, er . . . in love, I guess."

"Fair enough. What else?"

"I'm a terrible cook. Soup is one of the few things I *can* make."

"Not a problem. Anything else?"

"Yes. You owe me big. You're wearing a tux to the may-or's Christmas ball in two weeks. And you will be the most attentive, charming escort who ever attended a ball since the dawn of man. We're talking expensive dinner, corsage, boutonniere, champagne, limo, the works.''

"I will drink champagne from your slipper.''

Lauren wrinkled her nose in disgust. "Everything but that!''

"I'll make Miss Manners look like a pig,'' he promised solemnly. "You're not going to change your mind about this, are you? Get second thoughts in the cold light of day?''

"When I commit to something, I stick with it to the bitter end. I may kick myself for being stupid enough to try this outlandish farce, but no, I promise I won't do that to you. Or Abigail.'' Her voice softened at the mention of his grandmother. "Hopefully she'll be fine.''

Lauren was beginning to grow uncomfortable under David's unfathomable gaze. She wondered what he was thinking. "I guess I'll go put on a pot of coffee for our planning session. We'd probably better get that out of the way before tomorrow morning.''

David followed her into her French-country kitchen. "Good thinking, darling.''

Lauren shot him a pointed look.

"Just practicing. You have the same kitchen I do. Only yours is . . . nice.'' ·

"Yours is nice, too.''

"Nah, I know it has that early Salvation Army look, but I'm working on it.'' His upper body sprawled lazily across the countertop as he watched Lauren measure coffee into the filter. "So, what side of the bed do you sleep on?''

"David, I hardly think she'll ask *that*.''

He grinned. "I was just curious. So?''

"So . . . what?'' She filled the coffeepot with water.

"So, do you sleep in the buff?''

Lauren nearly dropped the pot. "Why on earth would that ever come up?''

"You never know. Besides, we're married. We know about each other's bedroom attire.'' He paused. "Well, at least I know about yours.''

She busied herself with the coffeemaker to hide her embarrassment. "I can see this isn't going to get us anywhere," she groused over her shoulder.

"I'm sorry. I'll be good."

"You're going to have to be, if we're going to pull this off." She turned around to face him. "We'll probably have to have to play most of it by ear. You know, take cues from each other."

"I'm not sure I follow."

"For example, when I talk about my family, you go along with what I say and act like you know them."

"Okay," he agreed cheerfully.

"I've never been married before, so I don't know exactly how to act, but it shouldn't be that hard. My folks are married, after all, and I lived with them for eighteen years."

"You're lucky." His expression was longing. "My folks were divorced when I was just a kid. They're...gone now."

"I'm sorry," Lauren murmured.

"It's all right. I had Gran." He seemed uncomfortable with her sympathy.

"How long have we been married?" she asked, to change the subject.

"Not too long. I don't want us to be boring."

"Somehow I think being married to you will be anything but boring." Lauren got two mugs out of her dishwasher.

"What shall you do for a living? We can't tell her you're on TV."

"Why not?"

"Because Gran has seen you on TV, but she lost that part of her memory. Telling her you're an anchorwoman may remind her you're not my wife, and she may have another attack."

"That doesn't make any sense ..."

"I don't care. We can't take chances."

"If it's all going to be this complicated, I don't think I can do it." Lauren was starting to feel panicky.

"It's okay, just be a housewife."

"She'll never buy that! I can't even cook!"

"How about a lawyer? We can say we met at work."

"But I don't know anything about law."

"Perfect. She'll think you're just another fast-talking shyster."

"Like you?" Lauren grinned. She filled his mug with coffee and handed it to him.

"Touché." He smiled into his cup.

The clock in the living room chimed midnight. A thick blanket of snow had muffled the city's noises and left a hush in its wake. Lauren felt as if they were the only two people in the world. Her cozy, warm kitchen was lit only by the single light glowing under the hood of her range. She was lulled by a growing sense of intimacy with her neighbor. Funny. She'd only known him a little over a week. It felt like years. *Some people you just seem to click with,* she thought. As if a missing piece of a puzzle had been found, Lauren felt complete when she was with David. It was a completeness she didn't get from her work, a completeness she'd never found with Joe. She batted the idea away in her mind. Of course she was complete. Wasn't she always busy? In demand? She was already getting carried away with this wife routine.

"I suppose it's time for bed." She looked over at David, who was sipping his coffee thoughtfully. "Here. By myself," she added when she noticed his raised eyebrows.

"No honeymoon?" he asked, teasingly. "You don't know what you're missing."

"I have a good imagination." She smiled, thinking back to their kiss.

"In that case, I'd better be going." His mouth curved ruefully as he set his mug down on the counter. "I really appreciate what you're doing for me, and for Gran. You're a special lady. I promise, I'll make it up to you at the ball. You won't be sorry."

"I have a confession to make," she admitted sheepishly. "I was going to the Bahamas with a . . . friend, but it was unexpectedly canceled at the last minute. I really don't have any special plans for my vacation time. In fact, I was beginning to feel a little bored. So I guess you're kind of do-ing me a favor.''

"Glad I could be of service." He went out of the kitchen into the living room and picked his keys up off her coffee table. "What time can you be over in the morning?"

"Is eight early enough?"

"That should be fine. We can get started on breakfast before Gran wakes up."

"Breakfast? I'm cooking?"

"We can't exactly go out, and you know how she feels about wives being able to cook."

"Better make it seven-thirty. Burn factor."

David laughed, pulled her front door open and stepped into the hallway. "See you in the morning." As he closed the door behind him, she could have sworn she heard him add, "honey."

David's hair was still damp from the shower when he an-swered his front door the next morning. Lauren was stand-ing in the hall in her pajamas and slippers, a wiggling Hairball in her arms.

"I thought we should strive for realism," she supplied, glancing down at her attire. "I'll bring some clothes and things over later, when she's napping."

"Perfect," he breathed, standing back to let her in. Hairball jumped out of her arms and immediately ran un-der his couch. How would he get through the day? Even with tousled hair and funky pajamas, she was sexy.

"Don't worry, he just used his litter box. I'll get that later, too," she assured him.

"No problem. So far, he's the model house guest."

Two shiny eyes peered suspiciously out at them from un-der the couch, and the tip of a fuzzy tail flicked angrily back and forth.

"I've already started the coffee. Want some?" he asked as he led her back to his kitchen.

She smothered a yawn with the back of her hand. "Yes." she looked up at him sleepily.

So, this is what Lauren Wills, anchorwoman, looks like in the morning, he thought, pouring her a steaming mug of fresh coffee. Not bad. He could learn to live with it.

"Okay. What do you want me to burn first?" She pushed her hair back, away from her face.

"I thought we could have fresh fruit, cold cereal, muffins and juice. That way, you just have to cut up some fruit. No cooking." He proudly held up a cantaloupe.

"Do you know first aid?"

"Yes." He looked puzzled.

"Good," she said, and took the melon out of his hand. "Where are your knives?"

"Um, hey. Idea. You set up her tray. I'll slice the fruit. I can only stand one patient at a time."

"That I can handle."

They had nearly finished preparing breakfast when Abigail's bell tinkled in her bedroom. Lauren looked at David in panic.

"What now?" she whispered.

"We serve breakfast, honey." He picked up Abigail's tray and winked at her conspiratorially. "It's showtime," he said, leaving her standing in the kitchen with her mouth open. Hurrying after David, she found him settling Abigail in with her tray. A tiny little bird with a gray bun—that was Lauren's impression of David's grandmother. Her heart lurched with compassion. Yes, she knew without a doubt that she was doing the right thing. Okay, maybe she had a few doubts. But one look at that sweet, bright-eyed little face, and they all seemed to melt away.

"Lauren, dear! I'm so glad to see you. How are you feeling this morning?" Abigail chirped.

She glanced nervously at David. "Much better... Gran. I'm so sorry I didn't say good-night last night, but I had such awful... cramps..."

David shook his head imperceptibly and pointed to his forehead.

"In my head. Oh, they were just awful. A migraine, sort of. Like a vise, just twisting—"

"But she's all right now," David said, interrupting her. "Isn't that right, sweetheart? After my special massage, well . . . you nearly passed out, you fell asleep so quickly."

Lauren turned to David in disbelief. Where was he going with this? She was definitely going to have to use some fancy footwork to keep this thing on an even keel. She wiggled her toes inside her slippers.

Abigail beamed at David. "Isn't that nice? I sometimes wake up in the middle of the night with the same sort of thing, and Bertie just sings me back to sleep. It's a very romantic way to cure a headache. You should try that sometime, David," she advised him knowingly.

"Yes, David *darling*." Lauren emphasized the endearment. "In fact, I'm sure we'd both enjoy it if you sang a little something for us now." They both looked at him expectantly.

Okay, he deserved to be put on the spot, he admitted to himself. Turnabout is fair play. But what was this about Bertie singing to Gran at night? Bertrand died nearly ten years ago. He was going to have to have a little talk with Homer about the man's intentions.

"Well?" Lauren smiled sweetly.

"I'm thinking!" he snapped. This was ridiculous. Who ever heard of singing to cure a headache? "I'm more of a shower singer, really, perhaps you'd like to join me there?" He gave her a crooked smile.

"Sing, David," she commanded.

"I gotta dee dee, I gotta dee dum, I gotta dee dee dee da da dum," he warbled badly.

Lauren groaned. "Stop! My headache is coming back."

Abigail tsked sympathetically. "I'm afraid it doesn't work for everyone. These muffins are marvelous! Don't let me keep you two from your breakfast. Go eat, we can chat later."

David poured Lauren a glass of orange juice, and sat down across the table from her.

"That went pretty well back there," he said, crunching his cereal thoughtfully. "Don't you think?"

"Sure, if you don't count that pathetic excuse for a song. And what was that about a special massage? Try to warn me before you go off chasing these kinky rabbits."

"You recovered beautifully. At my expense, too, I might add." He chuckled. "You really don't like my singing? I'm hurt!"

"Don't quit your day job," she quipped. "So, what's on the agenda for today, darling?" Lauren's eyes danced mischievously.

"Gee, honey, I don't really know." David leaned back in his chair and blew on his coffee. "Any ideas?" He grinned daringly at her.

"I was going to decorate my place for Christmas today, but since I'm here . . ." She let the sentence hang in the air.

"I don't have any Christmas decorations because I always spend the holidays with Gran. Every year, she goes all out. Why don't you bring your decorations over with your other stuff, and we'll put them up here? Gran loves that sort of thing." David's eyes were hopeful. She had the feeling that he liked that sort of thing, too, but wouldn't admit it.

"Good idea. Let's go check on her, and I'll run and grab everything I'll need for the next few days, or whatever."

They found Abigail fast asleep, with Hairball purring happily on her lap.

"I think Hairball has found a new love," Lauren whispered to David.

"Looks like the feeling's mutual," he agreed.

The pile at Lauren's front door grew steadily higher. Christmas decorations, litter box, cat food, cat dish, suitcase, books, games, a waffle iron, a curling iron, an iron skillet, an ironing board and an iron. One would think she'd been a Girl Scout, she mused, throwing a deck of cards on top of the mountain.

Just what exactly does one bring to a ludicrous situation like this? she wondered. Antacid? She headed to the bath-

oom and stuffed her overnight bag with aspirin and toilet
ies. Making a last-minute check of her bedroom, she picked
ıp the skimpy nightgown she usually wore and popped it in
he bag. It would look realistic hanging in David's bath-
oom, she thought. She smiled at the thought of him sing-
ng in the shower. This morning had actually been fun, she
eflected. Certainly more interesting than most of her dates
vith Joe. Lauren tried to conjure up an image of Joe in her
nind, and all she could come up with was a picture of Da-
ıd's ruggedly handsome face.

The doorbell broke her reverie. David stood lounging ca-
ually in the hallway. "Hi. You got the stuff?" His stage
vhisper was conspiratorial.

"Yeah, I got it." She winked broadly and held the door
ıpen for him. "Now we just need to stash it."

"Where? In a damn warehouse?" he asked, staring slack-
awed at her pile of supplies. "You weren't a Girl Scout at
ome point, were you?" he asked, picking up the waffle
ron.

She looked at him balefully. "Cut the snide remarks. We
lon't have much time. With our luck, she's probably al-
eady awake."

David's muscles bulged with effort as she loaded him up
vith all of her iron products.

"You really use all this stuff?" he asked in amazement.

"Yes, I really use all this stuff," she echoed defensively.

David was experiencing déjà vu. Hadn't he just been
hrough this with Gran? Between Gran's stuff and Lau-
en's stuff, there would be no room for his stuff.

"Women." He grunted under his breath.

"Pardon?" Lauren gasped as she dragged two large car-
ons of Christmas decorations into the hallway.

"Come on."

"I'm trying!"

"Just throw it anywhere." David instructed as they carted
he last load of clothing into his bedroom.

"I'm not *just throwing* my clothes anywhere," Lauren said severely. "I might never find them again," she added surveying David's messy bedroom.

He had the grace to look apologetic. "I, uh, haven't had much time to tidy up," he said, pushing back some of the clothes in his closet to make room for hers.

"I'll say. Don't let Gran in this room, or it will put her over the edge for sure."

He smiled at her unconscious use of his name for Abigail. She was really getting into this. He liked that about her. David watched Lauren gracefully step over a pile of his dirty laundry and begin hanging her clothes in his closet.

"I'll go see if she's up yet. Just make yourself at home." He waved his hands around. "Maybe I'll make a bed for her on the couch. She can help us decorate the tree."

"Good idea. I'll make some hot chocolate." She noticed his skeptical expression and laughed. "It's instant. How wrong can I go?"

After he left, Lauren walked thoughtfully around his room. Curious, she ran her hand over his sports trophies and peered at pictures of him posing with different athletic teams when he was younger. He'd been a cute boy. Skinny but cute. He certainly had filled out nicely. She glanced down at her hand and wiped it on her jeans. This place could use a good dusting. Turning, she looked down at the floor. This place could use a good sandblasting, she thought wryly.

The rumpled sheets on his king-size bed brought a sudden rush of tension to her very core. Inching closer, she could almost see him lying there, the sheets twisted around his naked torso. He *did* say he slept in the buff...didn't he? Knowing him, he did. Suddenly Lauren screamed.

"I'm sorry!" David said, jerking his hand off her shoulder. "I didn't mean to scare you."

Lauren's heart threatened to burst out of her chest and bounce off the ceiling. "No! It's okay!" She gulped. "I was, uh, thinking...."

"You must have been having some pretty deep thoughts." He looked over her shoulder at his bed, and then back down at her.

Their eyes met in a supercharged grip for what seemed like an eternity. His deep green eyes gleamed with invitation. Her breath quickened, and her cheeks grew uncomfortably warm. It felt as though he could read her mind. With incredible effort, she dragged her gaze from his.

"I'm, um, finished in here," she stammered. "We should probably get started on the decorating."

"I set Gran up in the living room. She's really anxious to help us decorate. It's a great idea. I'm glad we thought of it." He draped his arm casually around her shoulders. "Come on, she's waiting." Gently he steered her out of his bedroom.

Abigail was resting comfortably on David's couch. Several plump pillows were crowded behind her back, and a colorful afghan covered her frail body. Hairball was once again snoozing contentedly in her lap.

"Hello, Lauren dear," Abigail warbled cheerily. "We're going to decorate the living room for Christmas." She patted a spot on the couch beside her in invitation. Lauren perched awkwardly on the edge of the cushion and patted Abigail's frail hand affectionately.

"I see you have a new friend," she said, motioning toward Hairball, who'd flipped over on his back and was lying spread-eagled on her lap.

"Oh, Mr. Archibald and I are old friends. Aren't we, Archie?" She rubbed Hairball's exposed stomach, and he began to purr loudly.

Well, if Hairball didn't object to being called Mr. Archibald, then she guessed she wouldn't, either. Mr. Archibald. Where had she come up with that name? Sounded like some kind of prissy hairdresser. She stifled a giggle as the cat sat up abruptly and started grooming his round belly.

David raised a quizzical eyebrow in Lauren's direction and silently mouthed the words *Mr. Archibald?* She lifted her shoulders slightly in reply.

Pulling the flaps back on the first of Lauren's containers, he asked, "What all do we have here, honey? I can never remember." He hunted around in the tissue-wrapped depths of the box.

"Oh, Lambchop, you remember! That one is Christmas tree ornaments. We'll save it till we get a tree."

"Of course, Lovelump, how stupid of me to forget," he shot back.

"Why don't we start with this one, Sweetpea?" she volleyed. To hide her mirth, she rose and pulled a second box over to the couch. Abigail reached inside and pulled out several tissue-wrapped objects.

"Oh, this *is* fun!" Abigail exclaimed. "Just like Christmas."

Lauren and David exchanged a silent glance that seemed to scream, "It *is* Christmas, Gran!" They were getting pretty good at this nonverbal thing, she thought.

Abigail unwrapped the first object to reveal a Victorian Santa. "It's beautiful!" she breathed. "Reminds me of my girlhood. Let's put it right here where I can see it." She set it on the coffee table beside her. Hairball grasped the tissue paper with his paws and tore off a large mouthful. "No, no, Mr. Archibald!" Abigail scolded. "That's not good for you!"

Hairball stared at her blankly for a moment, then tore off another bite of paper.

"Good boy," she said, patting his head.

The rest of the day was spent in relatively peaceful camaraderie. Abigail regaled them with stories of Christmas past as David's living room was slowly transformed into Christmas present. The lyrics coming from the CD player truthfully informed them that the weather outside was frightening. It snowed steadily all afternoon, effectively shutting the city down. Heat from the crackling fireplace kept the living room cozily warm, and, strangely, Lauren was content to be snowbound with her new "family."

She sat on the floor, her feet tucked beneath her legs, happily stringing popcorn. David relaxed on the floor across from her, pulling the popcorn off the other end of the string and eating it.

"Honeybear, quit that or I'll break your arm." She smacked his hand in midtheft.

"But, Dollface, I'm hungry," he complained. "Besides, I'm all done decorating, see?" David held the last box upside down, and a ball of tissue tumbled out onto his lap. "Well, well, well. What have we here?" Unrolling the ball, he held up a sprig of mistletoe. Hairball stood on David's thighs and sniffed at the greenery. "What do you think, Archibald, old man? Does it work?"

"Meah." Hairy reached up and swatted at the mistletoe with his paw.

"Oh, no, you don't, Hair—er...Archie. I think I need to test-drive this myself. But first I need a victim."

Lauren's pulse picked up rapidly as he began to crawl on all fours toward her. He's going to kiss me again, she thought wildly. And, to her complete amazement, she wanted him to. Trembling, she stuck her finger with the needle she'd been using to string the popcorn.

"Ouch!" she yelped, looking down at the pinprick of blood that stained her finger.

"Oh, dear! David, run and get Lauren a Band-Aid. She's bleeding!" Abigail clucked.

"It's nothing really." Lauren popped the wounded digit in her mouth. "Weally. I'll wiv," she mumbled in embarrassment.

"Let Dr. David see," David said, pulling her finger out of her mouth. He examined the minor wound carefully before holding the mistletoe over it and gently kissing it. Molten lava slowly spread from her fingertip throughout her entire body. She watched in fascination as the muscles in his back played under the taut fabric of his T-shirt. It was hard to resist the urge to reach out and touch them with her free hand. Lifting his head, he looked at her and grinned. "Owie all better?"

She nodded mutely while he continued to crawl closer to her. *Oh, no. Oh, yes.* He straddled her lap with his thighs and held the mistletoe up in the air. His stomach brushed her cheek lightly as he leaned over her head to kiss Abigail's cheek. "Merry Christmas, Gran."

"David, you rascal. Get off your poor wife. Why, you're crushing her!"

"I am?" Squatting back down on Lauren's lap, he peered into her face. "I'm sorry, Lambchop." He laughed, and tweaked her nose.

Lauren looked into his eyes in confusion, and his smile faded. An enigmatic expression crossed his face, and for a moment he simply watched her. Slowly he raised the mistletoe over her head and lowered his mouth to hers. His warm, soft lips touched hers for a brief instant. He leaned back on his heels and lowered the mistletoe into her lap.

"Merry Christmas, honey." A look of yearning lingered in his eyes.

"Merry Christmas, darling." She echoed the lyrics that were coming from the CD player. This was Academy Award-winning stuff, she reflected. A pity their audience was too out of it to notice.

Later that evening, Lauren stood in the middle of David's kitchen and warily eyed the contents of his refrigerator. She might not be much of a cook, but he wasn't much of a shopper. How did one prepare dinner from a jar of hot peppers, assorted lunch meats and a six-pack of soda pop? One didn't, she sighed and opened the freezer. Bingo. Frozen dinners. She pulled out three Mexican Fiestas and preheated the oven.

Even concentrating on something as simple as cooking directions was impossible. She kept flashing back to David's little kiss under the mistletoe. One small kiss had her completely unglued. One small, powerful, electric, hair singeing kiss. Slamming the frozen dinners down on the counter, she reminded herself that this was just a game. Abigail would be well soon, and they could come clean. Get back to normal. *What was normal now?* she wondered, squinting at one of the brightly colored Mexican Fiesta packages. Bake at forty-five degrees for 350 minutes. That couldn't be right. At this rate, they wouldn't eat for hours.

"Oh, that man," she growled.

"David, let's watch the weather report. It should be starting soon." Abigail handed David the remote control. "Here, I can't make heads or tails of your cable box."

Lauren stepped into the living room just in time to catch him turning on the five-o'clock edition of her nightly news show. Edna was sitting at the anchor desk, introducing the hour's top story.

"Snow, snow, and more..."

Rushing over to him, she snatched the remote control out of his hand and clicked the program off.

"Dinner is ready," she announced brightly. "Mexican Fiesta."

"So soon? My, you're fast!" Abigail exclaimed.

David took the remote out of her grasp and turned the TV back on.

"Snow and storm advisory conditions throughout the area..." Edna continued.

"Bring it in here, honey, we're going to catch the weather report," he said distractedly.

Lauren grabbed the remote and clicked Edna off again in midsentence. "It's snowing. You don't need the *news* to tell you that." She sent him a meaningful look.

"I *do* if I want to know how *long* it's going to snow." His tone was patronizing. He clicked the TV back on.

"Our head meteorologist with a report..."

Lauren pulled the remote away from him and snapped the set off again. "But I made your favorite—Mexican Fiesta!" she prattled.

"Okay, chill out. We'll just watch the weather report, and we'll eat, I promise." He took the remote back and turned the TV on again.

"Right after this." Edna introduced a station break. To Lauren's horror, the first spot in the break was a station promo. "News you can trust, with Seattle's top anchor team, Ben Whitehall and Laur—" With sudden understanding, David clicked the set off and smiled broadly at a very pale Lauren.

"Mexican Fiesta, you say, honey? Let's eat! I'm starving."

Abigail's face was perplexed as she looked back and forth between the two of them. "What about the weather report?" she asked.

"It's snowing," they answered in unison.

"Just as well." Abigail commented. "I don't like that Edna woman. Puts me to sleep. I like the other one much better. What's her name? Oh, I can't think of it now, but she's *much* better."

When the dishes had all been washed and Abigail was down for the night, David and Lauren relaxed in the living room with a cup of coffee. Lauren's entire body ached as though she'd just run a marathon. Sipping her coffee, she looked at David thoughtfully. He was intoxicatingly handsome, in an altogether different way from Joe. Joe was handsome in a pretty, flawless, almost-too-perfect sort of way. David was handsome in an all-male, smolderingly sexy sort of way. He was sprawled out on the couch like a tired lion after a hard day in the jungle. Tiny lines crinkled around his eyes when he turned his head to smile at her.

"Sorry about the news show thing earlier. I wasn't thinking."

"It's all right. I just didn't want to have to explain...."

"I know." He propped his head up with his arm. "You were brilliant."

"Not really." She colored slightly. "Sorry about the frozen dinners. I never promised you a rose garden." She smiled weakly.

"What? They were great. I don't like my food too hot, anyway. Burns my tongue."

"David, they were still frozen."

"Exactly." He chuckled. "Just the way I like them."

"Right. Did you see the expression of Gran's face?" she asked with a giggle.

"I've never seen anyone use a steak knife to cut refried beans."

"She was so sweet about it. But when your fork bent, I thought I was going to lose it."

"So, next time you leave them in a little longer. No big deal." The warmth of his smile was reflected in his voice.

"Next time..." she mused. "David, do you think she's getting any better?"

"Time will tell."

"You're right." Setting her coffee cup down, she stood up. "I have to get going. What time should I be back tomorrow?"

"Same time as this morning is fine. Obviously I'm not going into the office tomorrow, so we'll just take it easy. I think, all things considered, that we did pretty well today."

"Yeah." Her smile was rueful. "All things considered."

Lauren entered her freezing-cold apartment and turned on the heat. Her answering machine's light was blinking. Pushing the playback button, she waited for the first message.

Beep. "Lauren? It's me, Polly. Why is your machine on? You must be in the tub or something. Anyway, I just called to see how you're weathering the storm—and, of course, I want a hunk report. Call me." *Beep.*

"Lauren, it's your mom. How is the vacation going? Have you seen your neighbor? I was just wondering how his grandmother was. Call me if you want, when you wake up or get done doing whatever you're doing.... Zach! That's enough! Your brother hopes you are having a good time. Bye, sweetheart." *Beep.*

"Lauren? It's Joe. Do you have my sunglasses somewhere at your place? I'm going to Switzerland now, for New Year's, and I can't find them.... So, how are you? Call me. Bye." *Beep.*

Lauren thought she'd rather chew tinfoil than listen to Joe's latest vacation plans. Shaking her head in disgust, she headed for her bedroom. Trust Joe to call about his stupid sunglasses. What had she ever seen in him? Exhausted, she flopped down on her bed and considered not returning any of the calls. Then, picking the phone up off her nightstand, she punched in Polly's number and pulled her comforter up under her chin.

Polly's agitated voice filled her ear. "Where the heck have you been?"

"It's a long story."

"Does it have anything to do with Mr. Wonderful across the hall?"

"Everything." Lauren proceeded to tell Polly about David's "proposal," purposely omitting the part about her ignominious fall at the front door.

"So that's where you were all day! Wow! How long do you have to play along?"

"I don't know."

"You don't think this is all some sort of scheme to get your money, do you? I saw this story on a talk show about this guy who used his little old granny to get dates. They'd con the victims into marrying him, and he and Granny would take all their money and split!" Polly's voice had risen to a fever pitch.

"Polly, he's a lawyer. Why would he want my money? Plus, Abigail is too out of it to handle any scheme more complicated than knitting."

"What if he's fooled you? Just be careful you don't end up another victim of the old 'Women Who Love Men Who Use Their Old Sick Grannies to Make Them Love Them and Then Leave Them' syndrome."

"Polly!" Lauren giggled. "By the way, Joe called."

"Really?"

"Yeah, left a message about some lost sunglasses. He says he's going to Switzerland for New Year's."

"I'm sorry, Lauren."

"Don't be. I'd rather be here," she said, and meant it.

"Good. When you get time, we need to shop for ball gowns."

After she and Polly hung up, Lauren decided that even though it was getting late, she'd better call her mother. There might not be time tomorrow.

"Hi, honey. Is anything wrong?" Charlotte's voice held concern.

"No, Mom. I'm sorry it's so late, but I just got home."

"You haven't been out in this weather, I hope?"

"Actually, I've been over at my neighbor David's place all day, helping out with his grandmother."

"Aren't you sweet!"

"Umm...Mom? Remember how I told you she'd had some sort of stroke? Well, she...uh, she thinks we're married."

"Uh-oh."

Lauren braced herself for a barrage of motherly advice.

"How'd you handle it, honey?" Charlotte asked gently.

"We played along with her. *Oh, Mom!*" Lauren wailed. "I don't know what else to do! The doctors say that a sudden shock could *kill* her. And, Mom, she is such a little doll. You should see her. She's all the family David has left in the world, and...Do you think I'm awful for lying?"

"Lauren, your father and I brought you up to be honest. You *are* an honest young woman, and we're proud of you. But sometimes, maybe, total honesty can be harmful. You can always tell her the truth when she's better."

"So you think I'm doing the right thing?"

"I don't know, Lauren, but I'd hate to think what would happen if you told her the truth now. At least this way you're giving her a chance to get well."

"Thanks, Mom."

"You're welcome. Let me know if I can do anything to help."

Lauren hung up the phone, too tired to move. I should get up and wash my face, she thought sleepily. I should brush my teeth and hang up my... She was asleep before she could finish the thought.

The next few days passed uneventfully. David and Lauren fell into the easy routine of a long-married couple. Lauren would slip over early in the morning, feed the cat and help David fix breakfast. After the meal, David would call his office to check in and catch up on the progress of his most recent cases. His computer was linked to the law office by modem, and his fax machine enabled him to keep up on his paperwork. Business was slow because of the bad weather, so he could knock off by noon every day and join Abigail and Lauren for lunch.

When Lauren was done with the breakfast dishes each day, she would read to Abigail until the elderly woman fell asleep. After lunch, the three unlikely family members would play the games that Lauren had so laboriously lugged over from her closet.

They argued about politics over Lauren's burnt popcorn and tepid cocoa—argued so loudly that Hairball retreated under the couch for an entire day. By Wednesday, the temperature had risen enough to melt a good deal of the snow, and many of the major roads were opened.

Rose and Homer both called several times to check on Abigail's health. Homer continued to reassure David that Abigail would regain her mental capacity in time, and that for now it would be best just to humor her.

That evening Abigail insisted that they watch *Casablanca* on cable TV. The old movies were "ever so much better than the drivel they put out today," she proclaimed, and instructed David to turn out the living room lights. With Abigail and Hairball taking up the sofa, David joined Lauren on the love seat until Abigail began to snore softly.

She woke herself up with a snort. "Oh, my! Goodness, I should be off to my bed." She wiggled her eyebrows at them. "That way you two can get to some serious neck-ing." She stood up and tottered out to the hall. "Yes, Bertie and I used to neck up a storm during the movies. What fun!" Disappearing down the hall, she called, "Good night, lovies."

Lauren looked at David and burst out laughing. "I suppose that's my cue to leave."

David shook his head and dragged her across his lap. "Oh, no, you don't. You heard her. She expects us to sit here and, I quote, 'neck up a storm.'"

Shaking with laughter, Lauren pushed at his chest and tried to sit up. "How does one neck up a storm?" she squealed, struggling in his firm grip.

He bounced her back down on the seat and looked at her with mock horror. "You mean you don't know? Oh, no, that won't do at all. I guess I'll just have to teach you."

"No way!" Lauren giggled, still trying to free herself from his grasp. "You remember our deal—no funny business!" She howled at his hurt expression.

"Lauren, you don't want to *kill* my poor old grand-mother, do you? We'd better do what she tells us." He nuzzled her neck playfully.

"What are you talking about? She's in the next room. She won't know."

"Sure she will. It's obvious to me that you've never experienced a *storm!*" He growled and rained kisses all over her slender neck.

When she grew still in his arms and sighed with pleasure, he drew away and looked at her, his expression deadly serious. "Maybe you're right," he said, releasing her. "We are definitely playing with fire here. I'm sorry." He smiled grimly. "I nearly forgot our deal there."

"Don't be." Lauren's answering smile was awkward. "You were just getting into the husband thing. It was good, really." And, before she could change her mind about their deal, she left.

That night, after Lauren had gone home, David called Homer.

"How's it going?" Homer asked jovially.

"So far so good... We've had a couple of close calls, but we've managed to keep her pretty calm."

"Close calls, huh?" Homer chuckled. "I can imagine. She's put you two in quite a predicament. Must have to do some pretty fast talking."

"For two people who have never been married, and have no desire to ever be married, we're pretty convincing. Lauren's been just terrific," David said proudly.

Homer hummed in amusement. "You'll probably be pretty glad when this is all over and you can have some peace and quiet again."

"And how!" David grunted. "These two women have more stuff.... You should see my bathroom. Looks like a damn lingerie store. Speaking of peace and quiet, are you still coming over tomorrow to take Gran to the doctor?"

"I plan on it, barring any unforeseen weather problems. Her appointment is at one in the afternoon, so I'll be there around eleven-thirty in the morning to pick her up."

"Great. I'm going in to the office to meet with a client tomorrow. When should we expect you home?" David pushed his fingers through his hair and rubbed his aching head. *What was with the "we" thing?* He was starting to sound like a husband. He'd had a bellyful of sour marriages in his career as a divorce lawyer. This marriage, even though it was all a farce, was beginning to get to him. *But why?* he wondered. The past few days spent with Lauren had been great, with the exception of one or two cold showers, he admitted to himself. It was almost as if he were starting to believe it was true.

It would never work, he chided himself. It hadn't even worked for his own mom and dad. She was in love with her career, and he—well, he was happy the way things were. No alimony. No child support. No broken heart.

"David?" Homer's voice broke through his drifting thoughts.

"Yes?" David's mind searched for clues to the conversation, which had continued without him.

"I said I'd have her back by early evening, and if she's up to it, I'll buy her dinner on the way home."

"I'm sorry, Homer, my mind was wandering. Sure, that will be fine. We'll see you tomorrow."

Homer arrived promptly at eleven-thirty in the morning to collect Abigail. David was already at the office, so Lauren was there alone to see them off.

"Lauren—" Abigail slipped her arm around Lauren's slender waist "—you remember David's grandpa Bertie? Though I can't remember when you two were together last..."

Homer winked at Lauren and kissed her on the cheek. "Lauren, my dear, it's good to see you looking so well."

"Thank you...er...Bertie." Lauren shrugged helplessly.

"Lauren has vacation this week, or she'd be at work with David now," Abigail explained. "That grandson of ours works far too hard," she said with obvious pride. "I hope you won't be lonely today, dear."

"Oh, no," Lauren hastily assured the small woman. "I've got plenty to keep me busy."

"We'll let you get to it then, my dear. It was nice...seeing you, Lauren." Homer's eyes twinkled.

In a flurry of hugs and goodbyes, they were gone. The long day loomed before Lauren like an endless black hole. With nothing better to do, she decided to clean house. Abigail expected David's wife to run a tight ship. And for that, Lauren planned on having lobster the night of the Christmas Ball.

"Better go rent a sandblaster," she told Hairball dryly.

"Meah."

"Hi, honey! I'm home!" David called, loosening his tie, as he came through the front door of his spotlessly clean condo.

"I'm in here!" Lauren called from the master bedroom. David rounded the corner into his bedroom to see Lauren's dirt-streaked face poke out from under the bed.

He laughed in amazement. "What on earth are you doing?"

"Cleaning," she replied, waving her rag. "I don't want Gran to think I'm a slob. You know how she feels about cooking and cleaning."

"I'm not a slob." His mouth curved in humor.

"David, you could rotate crops under your bed." She held up a dust bunny. "The soil is perfect for it."

"Busted," he said with a laugh as he unbuttoned his shirt.

"What are you doing?" she demanded.

"Getting undressed."

"Why?"

"Because the shower would shrink my suit."

Her mouth felt as dry as one of the dust bunnies under his bed. She couldn't help but stare at his smooth, well-shaped torso. His scratches had healed beautifully. The sound of the front door closing forced her to peel her eyes away from the view.

"Shhh! What's that?" Lauren cocked her head in the direction of the living room.

"Hello! We're home!" Abigail called.

"It's just Gran and Homer," he said calmly, unfastening his belt.

"Well, get dressed! They might see us!" she commanded in an urgent whisper.

"So what? We're married." He pulled his shirt free from his pants, stripped it off, wadded it up and threw it over her head.

"David!" she sputtered, wrestling with his shirt.

"Yoo-hoo!" Abigail's voice was closer. "Oh, you're in here! Bertie, come on. They're in the bedroom."

"Gran, you should be careful. You could have caught us in a compromising position," David chided her good-naturedly.

"In the middle of the day? Nonsense."

"Oh, come on, Gran. You were a young married once."

Lauren wiggled further under the bed to avoid leaping out and strangling David.

Homer's head appeared through the doorway. "Hello, David!"

"Hi, Ho—tie!" *Hotie?* Abigail seemed not to notice. David glanced down at Lauren, who was still under the bed. "How did the doctor's appointment go?" His voice was loaded with unasked questions.

"Fine," Abigail chirped airily. "He says I have recovered remarkably well from my little fainting spell. Says I'm fit as a fiddle." She tapped at her chest with her gnarled old fingers.

David looked at Homer for verification.

Homer nodded. "It's true. Physically, she's doing quite well, provided she keeps taking her medicine and gets some more rest. The doctor feels she should stay here for a while longer...and visit." He looked at David meaningfully.

"Of course. We've really been enjoying our visit together. Haven't we, honey?" He smiled down at Lauren.

"Oh, mmm, hmm!" She smiled absently up at them.

"Good!" Abigail's eyes were bright with excitement. "In that case, I suggest we celebrate my progress with a dinner party! I hope you don't mind—" she turned to David "—but I've taken the liberty of inviting Bertie over for dinner Saturday night. I thought we'd have Lauren's family join us." She looked down at Lauren expectantly.

Lauren's eyes grew round, and she looked wildly at David for support. Mentally she tried to send him a message. *No!* she screamed inwardly. *Not a dinner party! Not my family! Not my cooking!*

"We'd love to, wouldn't we, sweetheart?" David smiled magnanimously.

"Of course, Lambchop," she mumbled, slumping all the way down and letting her forehead thump on the floor.

Chapter Six

By four o'clock on Saturday, Lauren was ready for a nervous breakdown. David's kitchen resembled the aftermath of a nuclear holocaust. *Why, oh, why, had she decided to make lasagna?* It had seemed like such a good idea at the supermarket that morning. All day Friday, Abigail had excitedly helped her make plans for her little dinner party. Something simple, Abigail had said. Pasta was supposed to be simple, wasn't it?

Her head pounded as she searched the array of cookbooks laid out on the counter before her. How did one tell when the noodles were done? One cookbook advised throwing a strand of spaghetti at the wall. If it stuck, the pasta was done to perfection. It wasn't spaghetti, she thought with a shrug, but what the heck. Worth a try.

Peering down into the swirling mass of lasagna noodles, she fished out one slippery devil and hurled it at the wall. Her aim was more than slightly off. The noodle seemed to fly through the air in slow motion, and come to rest across David's head and ears as he entered the kitchen. The shocked look on his face gave rise to a burst of hysterical laughter in Lauren.

"What the hell is going on in here?" he demanded, peeling the errant noodle off his head.

"Oh! I'm sorry!" She swallowed her laughter. "I was testing the pasta. To see if it was done. It's done, I think...because it stuck," she explained lamely.

"Right." David slowly took stock of the dozens of pots, pans, jars, cans, utensils, spices and cookbooks that littered the war zone that had once been his kitchen.

"Are you sure you don't need some help in here?"

"No!" she said, too harshly. "I mean, I can handle it. I want to do this. Really. I still have two hours before everyone gets here. Why don't you straighten up the rest of the place?" Her eyes pleaded with him for understanding. This was something she had to do alone. A test. A challenge. The theme from *Rocky* swelled in her head.

"Okay." David looked down at her in amusement. "If it means that much to you. Just holler if you change your mind. I'm not a bad cook."

"Okay, but I think I'll be fine." She smiled winsomely up at him to hide her growing panic. David reached out, took her by the shoulders and firmly pulled her body to his. He bent his head down and touched the tip of her nose with his mouth.

"Mmm." He took a step back and regarded her thoughtfully. "Do I detect a hint of oregano in that sauce?"

"Get out of here!" she yelled, pushing him through the kitchen door. His laughter rang out in the next room as the door swung shut. She knew she was a mess. Damp tendrils of curling hair escaped the clip that held her tresses in a loose pile on top of her head. Sauce speckled her face and blouse like so many brilliant orange freckles. I must look like Measle Woman, she mused, looking disgruntledly down at her rumpled clothing. A hiss drew her gaze to the stove, where the bubbling mass of pasta was beginning to boil over.

"Oh!" she wailed loudly. Frantically she pulled drawers open, searching for a pot holder. Finding one in the last drawer, she yanked the pot off the burner. The acrid smell of burned noodles assailed her nostrils. "Damn, darn it, blast!" she shrieked in frustration.

"Everything okay, honey?" David's voice called in concern through the closed door.

"Just ducky-doodle, darling," she called back acidly. "Just dandy," she muttered in desolation to herself. How on earth had she gotten into this mess? In two short hours, she would play hostess to the most absurd dinner party since Lucy cooked dinner for Ricky's boss. She still couldn't believe that her family had agreed to this charade. They'd actually seemed excited about being drawn into this web of deceit. She'd never understand her family. Especially her mother.

"We'd love to come," Charlotte had enthused on the phone. "I'm glad to hear that she's improving. We've been so concerned."

"Mom, you do understand that she is still a little mixed up about things. She thinks you guys are her grandson's in-laws."

"Yes, Lauren. I understand. Don't worry. We won't do anything to shock her. When I was a girl, my grandmother would get confused toward the end. She would call me by my mother's name, and that sort of thing. Whenever we'd correct her, she would get so angry with herself. Well—" Charlotte sighed at the memory "—it just seemed kinder and less upsetting to let her think what she wanted. It didn't really hurt anything."

"You mean this kind of thing runs in our family?" Lauren moaned. "Great. Oh, well. I guess this whole mess will be good practice for when you start to lose it."

"Good attitude, Zach," Charlotte teased.

"Mom! That's not funny. Now, I'm serious. You guys have to behave. This is important. Speaking of Zach, are you sure he'll be okay?"

"Lauren, will you relax? He'll be just fine. He's really looking forward to your little party. When I told him about it after you called last night, he said 'he wouldn't miss it for all the babes in China,' and 'it sounds like a first-rate hoot.' That's a quote.''

"Mom, you tell him to be on his best behavior, or I'll tear his head off and feed it to the apes. This woman, she's special. I don't want anything to happen to her."

"Of course, darling. You can count on us. Do you want us to pick Polly up on our way?"

"That's a good idea. I'll call her and tell her you'll be there for her at five-thirty. Is that okay?"

"Yes. Good luck, sweetheart. Everything will be fine. You'll see. Can I bring anything?"

"No, Mom." She sounded breezily confident. "I'm just going to make something simple."

Simple. How wrong could she be? A test in quantum physics seemed more appealing. The hands on the clock were inching toward four-thirty.

"Spread a layer of ricotta cheese over a layer of lasagna noodles," the instructions read. I can handle that, she reasoned, spreading the noodles she was able to salvage in the bottom of the baking dish. Taking a spoonful of the ground-up cheese concoction, she attempted to spread it. They must be joking, she thought in dismay. The cheese stuck to the noodles, rolling and tearing them as she dabbed it in the pan.

Wiping at her itchy nose with the back of her hand, she decided on a new plan of attack. Scooping up a glob of cheese with her hands, she smeared and patted it into place, finger-painting-style. *Who said art class would never come in handy?* she gloated in triumph. Poking the torn noodles down, she viewed her work critically. It wasn't pretty. Maybe it would taste better than it looked, she thought hopefully.

Polly would die laughing if she were here. Lauren giggled, almost irrationally. But at least Polly would know how to make lasagna. No wonder she'd sounded so excited about coming to this dinner party. It wasn't often one had a chance to laugh one's behind off.

Polly had accepted eagerly. "A dinner party? *You're* cooking? Of course I'll be there! I wouldn't miss it."

"Thanks, Pol," Lauren had breathed in relief. "I need all the moral support I can get."

"And your folks will be there too?" Polly had sounded amazed.

"Yes, and Gran's friend, Homer. She thinks he's her late husband, Bertie. It's very confusing, and you never know what she's going to say next, so just roll with the punches," Lauren advised her nervously.

This was never going to work. Maybe it wasn't too late to call the whole thing off. She could develop a sudden case of the flu. No. She couldn't disappoint Abigail. This dinner party was all she'd talked about since Homer brought her home from the doctor. Abigail had babbled on and on about how wonderful it would be to have the whole family together again. Just like old times. If this was like old times, Lauren wondered how the woman had managed to live so long. The stress was killing her.

"Now, let me get this straight." Polly was evidently trying to organize the jumble of information Lauren had given her. "Homer is Bertie, Hairball is Mr. Archibald, you are Mrs. Barclay, attorney-at-law, David is your husband, and your folks are his in-laws. Am I straight so far?"

"Right."

"Who am I? Every sitcom has a wacky neighbor. Can I be the wacky neighbor? You can call me Peggy!" she said, giggling.

"No! I need at least one person to just be herself." A note of desperation had crept into Lauren's voice.

"Shoot. That sounds boring." Polly was clearly disappointed. "Can't we at least say I have an interesting career? How about an international spy? Mafia ringleader? Belly dancer?"

"No, no, no! Pol, I'm counting on you!"

"Okay, okay. You're sure I can't bring anything?"

"No, I'm making something simple. It'll be a snap."

* * *

Snap. Snap, snap, snap. The microwave crackled and popped. Lauren opened the door and tentatively poked a fork into the sizzling ground beef. Shoe leather. No, shoe leather was too tender. Make that concrete. This just got worse by the minute. Dropping the fork, she slumped against the counter and tried to quell the sob that threatened to break her last shred of composure.

She sniffed and wiped her nose on her sleeve. The clock read nearly five. One hour left. Dully she reached into the microwave and withdrew the brick of molten lava that had once been ground beef. Spices. That was what this needed. Spices. A pinch of this, a dash of that, and a few handfuls of the other for good measure.

David's encouraging voice wafted through the door. "Something sure smells good in there, honey."

"Shut up!" she flung back. "Leave me alone, *honey!*"

"Sorry, Lauren." His sympathetic tone was her undoing. The door slowly opened, and his gorgeous, virile body filled the doorway. She tried to swallow past the huge lump that had lodged in her throat. Letting her shoulders fall dejectedly, she met his empathetic gaze with tear-filled eyes.

"It's... it's t-te-terrible," she choked.

David strode over and pulled her into his comforting arms. His warm body felt like a wonderful haven of strength. She pressed her cheek into his firm chest, and proceeded to soak the front of his crisp cotton shirt with her tears. Gently he caressed the back of her head and neck with his fingers, soothing away her tension.

"Oh, sweetheart," he murmured, rocking her back and forth. "It can't be that bad." He tilted her head up and wiped a tear from her cheek.

Lauren's voice came in ragged gasps. "It... i-i-is! I c-c-can't serve th-this mess!" She hiccuped. "What are we going—hic—to do?" Her large, watery blue eyes pleaded with his for an answer. She glanced around the room and began to cry again. "I just wanted everyth-th-thing to be perfect."

"Honey, don't you know it already is? How many women would give up their vacation to throw a dinner party for a little old lady they hardly know?" He tightened his embrace and rested his chin on the top of her head. "You've risen above and beyond the call of duty, and it means more to me than you'll ever know." He lowered his mouth and kissed her forehead. "You're a very special woman, Lauren. I've never known anyone quite like you." Tenderly he kissed each of her damp eyelids.

She brought her face up and looked at him searchingly. "You're not mad?" she gulped.

"Why would I be mad? So you've had a minor setback. We'll manage."

His warm, soothing voice calmed and excited her at the same time. The feel of his hard body pressed tightly against her soft one sent small lightning bolts of excitement from the top of her head to the tips of her toes. She nestled more closely into his comforting embrace. It would be so easy to fall in love with this man, she thought, and nuzzled his neck with her nose. He felt so good. He was so sweet. She planted a few tiny kisses under his ear and down around his jaw.

He stiffened slightly and pulled back. Looking down at her, he smiled ruefully.

"Sweetheart, as pleasant as this is, if we don't stop, I won't be held accountable for what happens next." Raw desire smoldered in the dark green depths of his eyes.

"Oh. Of course," she said, taking a jerky step back, embarrassed by her bold behavior. She was taking this wife thing way too far.

"Why don't you go shower, and get all gussied up? I'll handle this."

"I don't know," she said doubtfully, looking around.

"Go," he commanded, pushing her toward the door. "Go."

Smiling and shaking his head, David watched Lauren set off for the shower. She was really something. Sweet and selfless, yet she had fire. He sensed a passion that ran deep beneath her polished surface. A passion he wouldn't mind exploring. Hell, any woman who would help him with this crazy problem just might be a woman worth hanging on to. Even if she couldn't cook, he amended, warily looking around at the demolition area he had once called a kitchen. Picking up a dishrag, he threw himself into cleaning up.

Lauren felt much better after a scalding-hot shower. David was right. Everything would be okay. It had to be. Hurriedly she dressed in her new pale blue silky pantsuit. Pushing the soft sleeves of her jacket up to the elbow, she adjusted her shoulder pads and slipped her feet into matching blue pumps.

She brushed her hair till it shone with highlights, added finishing touches to her makeup and put on a pair of sparkling sapphire earrings. Surveying her reflection in the mirror, she decided she'd pass. Not bad for a half hour's work. And there was still thirty minutes till blast-off. A twinge of nerves fluttered in her stomach. Stage fright. With a deep breath, she headed back to the kitchen.

Thank God Gran is napping, David thought in frustration. Only a half hour left, and he still had to dress. There was nothing he could do about the lasagna, but at least now they had a green salad and some garlic bread. How did Harriet Nelson do it? Dinner on the table, a spotless kitchen, and all done in a crisp housedress with a strand of pearls at her throat. Real life was so much more complicated. He wiped his sweaty brow with a paper towel.

The sink was filled with dirty dishes, and he had yet to mop the sticky floor. No wonder Lauren was close to hysterics. He was feeling the strain himself.

"Hi," she said tentatively, coming into the kitchen. Gone was the sweet look of empathy with which he'd sent her to the bathroom. In its place was the frazzled look of a bachelor in over his head.

"You're back!" he barked. "Good. The salad's in the fridge, the bread is ready for the oven, and I need a shower." Without a backward glance, he shot out of the room like a man possessed.

Lauren tried to shrug off the disappointment she felt when he didn't comment on her new outfit. It's not like we have a real relationship, she told herself. It was just for show. Temporary. Nothing serious. She glanced at the clock on the wall. Twenty minutes and counting. Wearily she set the oven temperature to five hundred degrees and popped the lasagna and bread inside. The dishes could wait till morning, she decided. No one would come into the kitchen. After a thorough search of David's cupboards, she managed to find eight matching plates and started to set the table.

"Lauren, dear, what can I do to help?" Abigail, looking fresh from her nap, came into the dining room, where Lauren was trying to arrange a centerpiece over a stain in the tablecloth.

"Nothing, Gran!" she said with false gaiety. "Everything's under control." The nerves in her stomach were strung as tight as a violin.

"In that case, I'll stay out of your way. I'll be in the living room if you need a hand." She bustled over toward the doorway and paused. "I'm so excited!" She fiddled with the brooch at her throat. "You are such a dear to have this lovely dinner party for me. I can't remember the last time I looked forward to anything this much! Thank you," she said sincerely, and went into the living room.

Lauren watched the tiny woman in the brilliant flowered dress leave the room. The dinner party meant so much to her. The musicians in her stomach began to tune their instruments. One by one, the strings tightened. She went back into the kitchen, and looked at the clock. T minus ten minutes.

David bounded back into the kitchen and looked at her anxiously. "Are you all right? Did anything explode while I was gone? What should we do now?" The sheer velocity at which he fired the questions made her head reel.

"Yes. No. I don't know," she was finally able to answer. "Will you calm down? I'm the one that's having a nervous breakdown."

She watched him finger-comb his still-wet hair, and was suddenly aware that this dinner was just as important to him as it was to her. And he was just as nervous. He looked so cute, standing there in his softly faded blue jeans and cowboy boots. His black cotton dress shirt gave him an air of dark mystery. He looked great. Except for...

"David, what's wrong with your collar?"

"What?" He brought his hands up and felt it clumsily.

"You've got your shirt buttoned in the wrong holes." She bit her lower lip, trying not to smile.

"Oh." He grinned sheepishly. "I was in a hurry." He pulled his shirt out of his waistband and unbuttoned the buttons. Her eyes followed his hands as he slowly exposed his flat stomach. They trailed the line of dark hair that ran down from his chest and disappeared beneath his navel. *Oh, my,* she thought as she picked up a pot holder and began to fan herself.

"Lauren?" He was looking at her quizzically.

"Yes?" she squeaked, her mouth dry, as she tore her eyes away from his stomach and looked up in embarrassment.

"Lauren...do I smell something burning?" He was sniffing the air curiously.

Her embarrassment quickly turned to mortification. Large black clouds of smoke were belching out of the oven's belly.

"Oh, my! *Oh, my!*" was all she was capable of uttering.

David, however, was not at a loss for words. Cursing the questionable parentage of the appliance, he leaped into action. Flames shot out, singeing the hair on his arms, as he pulled the oven open. Lauren screamed harmony to his chorus of curses. He stripped his dress shirt off and began beating at the fire with it. Somewhere Lauren had heard that the best thing for a kitchen fire was flour. Or was it salt?

She ran over to the kitchen counter and grabbed the nearest canister. Prying the lid off, she judged the distance, took aim, and fired. The smoke detector chose that precise moment to detect smoke and blew a window-shattering whistle. Missing her mark, she managed to cover the half-naked David, and her new pale blue silky pantsuit with a thorough coating of flour.

"What the *hell* are you doing?" David bellowed above the shrill shriek of the smoke detector. His red eyes blazed angrily out of his flour-covered face. "The fire is *out!*"

With one swift, graceful movement, he reached up, tore the offending noisemaker off the wall and hurled it to the floor. Emitting one last, pitiful death scream, it landed, bounced once, and died.

Lauren pulled her fingers out of her ears and slowly opened her eyes. "You don't have to yell at me. I was just trying to help."

"Help?" he roared. "Help? When I want your *help,* I'll ask for it!" He wiped his face with what was left of his shirt. "I had it under control," he bit out angrily.

"Did not," she snapped defensively.

"Did too."

"Did not!"

"Did too!"

"Did not! Did not! Did *not!*" she yelled.

Nose-to-nose, they stood glaring at each other.

"Are we interrupting...something?" Charlotte asked tentatively.

Startled, Lauren and David jerked around to find six pairs of eyes staring in fascination at the scene in front of them. David pulled Lauren roughly into his arms.

"Hi!" he said blithely. "We didn't hear you come in! We were, uh...just putting the finishing touches on dinner, weren't we, sweetheart?"

"Yes!" She elbowed David in the ribs. "It's finished now!"

"Awesome!" Zach breathed.

"Would anyone like a martini?" Homer asked hopefully. A chorus of yeses followed him into the living room.

"What now?" Lauren asked wearily, looking up at David. "You look like you've just survived a major earthquake," she added with a grin.

"Barely." He grasped her hand and tugged her toward the door. "Come on, Mrs. Barclay, we'd better go change."

Lauren hung back. "Where?"

"In our room—where else?" he answered, pulling her down the hallway toward his bedroom.

"Do you think this is such a good idea?" she whispered. "My parents are out there, for pity's sake."

David drew her into the room and locked the door. "Get real, Lauren. I doubt they think we invited them over to kill time while we swing from the chandelier."

Lauren smiled. "Okay, you're right. You pick out fresh clothes for us, and I'll hop in the shower. Then you shower while I dress."

Clouds of steam rolled out of the bathroom as David slid open the closet door and went through her clothes. What was this? He pulled out a strapless red minidress. "Now we're cookin'," he murmured triumphantly, and found a pair of high-heeled pumps to match. Tossing the dress on his bed, he tentatively searched her drawer for clean underthings. What on earth was this? he wondered, holding up a lacy bustier and trying to envision Lauren in it. She had great taste in underwear—that much was crystal-clear. Untangling a skimpy pair of French-cut panties and a garter belt, he laid them on the dress. He tossed on a pair of sheer nylon stockings for good measure. This was fun! Uncertainly, he dug out a see-through underwire bra. She'd definitely need this. His large hands wrestled with the hooks, which were caught on another interesting, yet unidentifiable, piece of underwear.

"What are you doing?" Lauren, wrapped in a huge bath sheet, stood in the doorway and watched him, trying not to laugh.

He pitched the bra onto the pile he'd assembled for her. "I'll just go get ready...." he mumbled on his way to the shower.

Lauren smiled broadly at his choice of clothing. He obviously hadn't had Abigail's health in mind when he'd chosen her outfit. She could hear him singing in the shower as she dried her hair and slipped into a conservative gray wool dress.

"Ba dee dee dee da!" he shouted. He really was a bad singer, she mused. Struggling with her zipper for several minutes, she didn't notice David come up behind her.

"Allow me," he whispered, lifting her heavy tresses out of the way and easily zipping her dress.

"Thanks," she murmured, and turned around, avoiding eye contact with him in his current state of undress.

"You look great." He grinned. "Decided not to go with the red dress?"

"Another time," she promised, stepping into the bathroom, where she struggled to bring her breathing under control. His damp towel came sailing past her to land on the shower floor.

"Oh, my-gosh," she groaned, and splashed cold water on her face. Now he was standing out there *naked!* Good Lord, and her parents were in the next room. Gulping down two aspirins, she began to reapply her makeup.

"So that's how it's done," David said, watching her coat her eyelashes with mascara. "I thought you were naturally beautiful," he added teasingly, and quickly combed his hair. "I'm ready if you are." He kissed her lightly on the cheek. "Off to battle."

"Off to battle," she echoed weakly, and sped back to the living room with David to join the party in progress.

"Ah, David, my boy!" Jack clapped him soundly on the back. "Good to see you!" He pumped David's hand enthusiastically.

"Thank you, sir... um, Dad." David grinned at the mischievous twinkle in Jack's eye.

"And Lauren! Honey, it's good to see you looking so well. Married life certainly agrees with you." Jack was obviously enjoying his role.

Polly seemed equally eager to jump into the fray. "I'll say," she said, moving up to join Jack and David. "Why, she positively glows. Funny, but it seems like just last week she was dating Joe. How time does fly." She smiled at David appreciatively. "Our Lauren has certainly done well for herself."

It was clear to Lauren that Polly was taken with her new husband. She was eyeing him as if he were some kind of super hero, Lauren noticed irritably. The others, finished with their conversation about the inclement weather, stopped talking to listen.

"So, what's for dinner, sis?" Zach asked loudly. "I could eat a horse. I can't wait to eat one of Lauren's home-cooked meals. She's such a *good* cook," he added to Abigail and Homer, plainly relishing Lauren's discomfort.

David smiled at Lauren knowingly. "She sure is. I bet I've put on ten pounds since the wedding."

"You wear it well, David," Polly gushed adoringly. "I'd never have guessed you'd gained any weight at all. You don't look any different than the day I met you."

Lauren suddenly needed air. "I think I'll just check on dinner." She excused herself and rushed into the kitchen. She hadn't thought it was possible for her spirits to sink any lower than they already were, but they did. The kitchen should be condemned, she thought, surveying the charred remains of what was supposed to have been their dinner. Eyeing a butter knife, she contemplated her wrists. The kitchen door opened behind her, and Charlotte, carrying two large bags, came in to stand beside her daughter.

"This brings back memories," she said, smiling fondly at the mess in the kitchen.

"Oh, Mom! What was I thinking? I can't cook!" she moaned in despair. "What am I going to do?"

"Well, I had a feeling something like this might happen, so I brought plan B." She set the bags down on the counter. "I hope everyone likes chicken," she said, pulling a barrel of mouth-watering fried chicken out of the bag. Rolls, potatoes and gravy, corn on the cob and coleslaw followed.

Lauren was weak with relief. "Oh, Mommm!" she groaned. "I owe you!"

"Nonsense, darling." Charlotte waved her slender hand airily. "My first company dinner was a disaster, too. You come by it naturally. Give it time. You'll learn."

"Mom, you *do* realize we're not really...married." Lauren caught Abigail entering the kitchen out of the corner of her eye. "To our jobs," she finished quickly. "No, work definitely comes second." Pushing the barrel of chicken behind her back, she turned to smile at Abigail.

"Lauren, dear, is there anything I can do to help?" Abigail's face registered mild surprise at the state of disarray in the kitchen. "Help you clean up or something?" she asked.

"No, I think I pretty well have things under control here. Would you mind telling everyone dinner will be ready in a few minutes?"

"Certainly, dear." Abigail stepped over the mangled smoke detector on her way out.

Charlotte was busy hunting for the few remaining clean serving dishes and loading them with the fast food. "I can see why you're so taken with her," she murmured to Lauren. "She's awfully cute. I can also see why you're so taken with her grandson. He's awfully cute, too."

"Mom!" Lauren was shocked.

"Close your mouth, honey. Soup's on." Charlotte carried several serving dishes to the dining room and announced that dinner was ready.

David sat at one end of the table, Lauren at the other. Abigail was seated between Zach and Jack on one side, and Homer was between Polly and Charlotte on the other. David stared at the dish of chicken in his hand.

"Lauren, you never cease to amaze me," he commented dryly.

"Yes, dear, I do believe this is the best fried chicken I've ever tasted," Abigail put in.

"Thank you," Lauren said demurely.

"Yes, Lauren," Polly interjected. "This chicken is wonderful. I must have the recipe."

"It's an old family secret," Lauren gritted out through clenched teeth.

Zach guffawed. "Yeah, eleven herbs and spices."

"That many?" Polly asked in mock wonder. Reaching over, she patted David fondly on his arm. "I can remember a time when Lauren couldn't cook worth beans. And now she's so *domestic!* Ain't love grand?" She beamed at the group in general.

Everyone cheerfully agreed—nodding and grinning like a bunch of boobies, Lauren thought in dismay. What was with these people? This was no game! This was serious business. At this rate, someone was going to get too carried away with his or her role and blow the whole thing. No telling what would happen when Abigail figured out the ruse. Lauren wondered what she would do if Gran collapsed, facefirst, into her coleslaw. Frantically she tried to remember her CPR.

Cold beads of sweat collected on her brow. She glanced around the table, not hearing the conversation that surrounded her. Was she the only sane person here? The only one who understood the severity of the situation? Even David seemed oblivious of the fact that this thing could get out of control. He was literally basking in Polly's approval, and it was clear that Zach worshipped him. A far cry from the way they used to treat Joe. And her parents were no help, either.

Charlotte and Abigail were prattling away about babies, and Jack and Homer were deep in some discussion about— Whoa! Back up. A snippet of the conversation about babies stopped Lauren's woolgathering. What was the question? She looked around the table to find everyone focused on her. David looked suspiciously uncomfortable.

"Is it true, Lauren? Abigail tells us you and David are trying to start a family." There was a certain amount of parental censure in Charlotte's question.

"I... Well, I..." She looked furiously at David for a way out of this new turn of events.

He shrugged and smiled weakly at her. Pretending to be married was one thing, but pretending to have a baby was out of the question.

"So, the Laurster has a bun in the oven! Outrageous!" Zach looked at David with new respect. "And I thought this was just another one of her boring vacations."

Polly jumped in to cover for Zach. "I thought you looked awfully pale tonight. That explains everything." She looked at David wisely. "Someone in her condition shouldn't be slaving away over a hot stove all day."

"Now hold on just a minute here!" Lauren sputtered. "I think there has been some kind of misunderstanding."

"Yes, she's right. There is a difference between *trying* to start a family and actually *starting* one," David explained. "We thought we'd wait on the family thing.... Right, honey?"

"Right. Yes, we want to wait. Until we've been... married, for a while."

Charlotte was as visibly relieved as Zach and Abigail were plainly disappointed.

"That makes good sense, kids. Don't want to get the cart before the horse." Jack munched a drumstick thoughtfully. "Though, as I recall, the trying part can be enjoyable." He winked at David.

"Jack!" Charlotte was scandalized.

"What? They're married. We're all adults."

Charlotte opened her mouth, closed it, opened it, then apparently thought better of it and closed it again. "They *would* have beautiful children," she reflected.

"Mom!" Lauren went pink.

"I wanna be an uncle," Zach whined petulantly.

"Hey, I wouldn't *mind* trying, Lord knows." David raised his eyebrows suggestively at Lauren and then turned to Charlotte. "But she's pretty insistent that we wait."

Lauren pasted a brittle smile on her face and hissed at David through her tightly clamped jaw. "Sweetheart, could I see you in the kitchen?" Her eyes bored into his with determination.

"Sure, babe." He excused himself and followed her into the kitchen. "What's up?"

"What's up? I'll tell you what's up!" She pushed her forefinger into his chest to emphasize each word. "This whole thing is getting out of control! Now we're working on having a baby?" Her voice rose shrilly. "I only have two weeks of vacation here! Just how is having a baby supposed to help Gran get well?" Tears gathered in her eyes and threatened to rain down her bright pink cheeks. "David, I'm scared!"

Lauren stood, her body vibrating with fear, her eyes pleading with his for some kind of help.

What a jerk, David berated himself as he realized Lauren was in the beginning phases of a nervous collapse. He'd been enjoying himself so much, he'd forgotten the strain she'd been under all day. Suddenly feeling incredibly selfish, he groaned and pulled her into his arms, where he whispered soothing words and stroked her quivering back.

"I'm so sorry," he murmured. "You're right. Sometimes I get carried away. But, honey, you make it so easy. You're doing such a good job, I tend to forget that we're not really married."

"Oh, sure." She sniffed into his chest. "You're just saying that to make me feel better."

Leaning back, he smiled into her eyes. "Lauren, I'm saying it because it's the truth. Gran is having a wonderful time. And, if I'm not mistaken, so is everyone else. You are doing an incredible job, and I couldn't be prouder if you were my wife."

"Really?"

"Really." He pulled her hands from around his neck and kissed her palms. "Come on, let's go finish that delicious dinner you worked so hard on."

Polly and Charlotte helped Lauren clear the table when they had all consumed the last of plan B. Everyone else retired to the living room for more conversation and some of Homer's after-dinner libations.

The Mad Hatter's tea party was nearly over, Lauren thought with relief as she pulled the ice cream cake she'd bought that morning out of the freezer. Now, let's just make it through dessert. She crossed her fingers for luck.

"He is gorgeous!" Polly burst out once all three women were safely in the kitchen, out of earshot of the others. "Lauren, you are so lucky! I'd give anything to have Gus look at me the way he looks at you."

"What way is that?" Lauren looked curiously from Polly to Charlotte.

"So possessive. The man is obviously in love with you!" Polly nearly swooned.

"Watch those plates, Polly. I can't handle any more kitchen disasters. And he's not in love with me. This is all just an act. He's only doing it for his grandmother's sake. Once she's well and comes to her senses, he'll forget I'm alive."

"I wouldn't count on that, honey. I agree with Polly. The man is positively smitten with you."

"Oh, Mom, be serious! He's desperate. Desperate times call for desperate measures. I happen to know that he is dead set against the institution of marriage. And I don't blame him. You should hear some of the horror stories he tells me about his clients, not to mention his own parents' awful divorce. Besides, he knows how I feel about it. When would I ever have time to have a family? It wouldn't be fair to anyone."

Polly and Charlotte exchanged small knowing glances. "Yes, dear. Whatever you say."

"I wish you two would knock it off. I mean it. This is just an act." Lauren eyed them both sternly. "An enjoyable act, I'll admit." She grinned. "But an act nonetheless. Soon everything will be back to normal."

"Sure, Lauren, sure," Polly agreed. "Back to normal."

"Just serve the dessert, please."

David poked his head into the kitchen. "Anyone need rescuing in here?" His lips twitched mischievously.

"No." Lauren pretended to be insulted. "Except maybe from your mother-in-law."

"Who? Oh, right! Mom!" He took the plates out of Charlotte's hands. "So, what are you doing to my sweet wife?" he asked teasingly.

"Just trying to talk some sense into her, honey. Give those to Homer and Zach. I'll bring the rest." She followed David out of the kitchen.

"So, just what is it you want to do after college, young man?" Homer asked Zach as Lauren took her place on the couch next to David.

Zach looked up at him from the floor, where he'd squeezed his large frame under the coffee table. "I've been thinking about following Lauren's footsteps and becoming a—" he paused for dramatic effect, and Lauren could have sworn her heart stopped beating "—lawyer." He grinned at her. "She's always been sort of a role model for me."

"Law school?" Jack seemed pleased. "Why haven't you mentioned this before?"

"I don't know. It just sort of came to me out of the blue." Zach set his plate on the floor for Hairball to polish. "Lauren made it look so easy. Like one day, *poof!* She's a lawyer! And if she can do it, heck, anyone can." He leaned back on his hands and shook his long mane over his shoulders.

"Lauren, what made you decide to become a lawyer?" Abigail asked.

Lauren felt David squeeze her knee reassuringly. "I don't know that I ever made a conscious decision. It just seemed to happen to me."

"Lauren always was career-minded. Even when we were kids," Polly added. "Her Barbie doll always carried a tiny briefcase, and Ken was always her secretary. That's why it came as such a shock when she announced her marriage plans to David."

Jack swallowed the last of his dessert. "Could have knocked me over with a feather," he said affably. "But her mother and I couldn't be more pleased."

"Nor I." Abigail smiled fondly at Lauren. "Lauren has been such a blessing to us all."

David planted a husbandly kiss on the top of her head. "I don't know where I'd be without her," he said appreciatively.

Lauren shifted uncomfortably at the turn in the conversation. "Would anyone care for more coffee?"

"Oh, not for me, dear. It's past my bedtime already." Abigail did her best to stifle a yawn. The excitement seemed to have worn her out.

"We should be going, anyway." Charlotte stood and began collecting the dessert plates.

Homer glanced at his watch. "My! It's later than I thought. I'd probably better head out myself." Turning to Abigail, he kissed her gently on the cheek. "Keep up the good work, my dear. You seem to be making wonderful progress. At this rate, you'll be good as new and back home in no time."

"Oh, Bertie! Don't go acting like you miss me, now." She batted at his arm playfully. "I've truly been enjoying my visit with the kids. It's been wonderful therapy for me. Although—" her eyes twinkled "—I'm sure they'll be glad when I'm strong enough to go home. Young married people need time alone together."

"I'll bet you've been a delightful houseguest, Abigail." Charlotte hugged the small woman lightly.

Hugs and handshakes were given all around, and Abigail, weary from the commotion, took herself off to bed.

"Thank you for a delightful and interesting evening." Homer squeezed Lauren's hand warmly. "Don't believe I've enjoyed myself so much in years." He smiled at the group in general. "Nope. Haven't seen so many people work so hard for a common cause since the First World War." He saluted jauntily, and disappeared down the hall.

Polly hugged David enthusiastically. "David, let's not go so long between visits!" she joked.

He ruffled her curly mop. "It does seem like forever."

"David. Dude. Welcome to the family, homey. You are definitely the pick of the litter." Zach high-fived David on his way out the door.

"Thanks, Bro."

"Thanks, Mom, thanks, Dad. For everything." Lauren released her parents and unconsciously went to stand close to David. "You saved our behinds."

David put his arm around her shoulders and squeezed. "You sure did. Gran had a great time. I owe you both." He grinned devilishly. "If you ever need a divorce, it's on me."

Charlotte kissed him on the cheek. "Jack, could we ask for a better son-in-law?"

"No, honey. He's all right in my book." Jack shook hands heartily with David. "Take good care of my little girl, young man." His voice held a friendly warning.

"The best, sir. And thanks again."

"Anytime. Glad we could help."

Lauren closed the door and sagged against it tiredly. "I should probably do the dishes," she groaned.

"They'll wait. This won't."

"What won't?"

"This." He took her hand and drew her over to the doorway where he'd hung the mistletoe the week before. He looked up at it and pulled her directly underneath it and into his arms. He sighed heavily with frustration.

"I thought they'd never leave. I've been wanting to do this all night. All week. Hell, I've wanted to do this again since the night I proposed to you."

Lauren's breath quickened, and her entire body began to tingle. "So what's stopping you?" she murmured, lost in the powerful desire she saw reflected in his expression. His strong hands tilted her head back gently.

"At this moment, nothing on earth." He brought his mouth within a hairsbreadth of her gently parted lips. "Nothing," he repeated hoarsely.

She wound her arms around his neck and filled her hands with the thick hair at the back of his head. His kiss deepened, and he spread his legs slightly for support. Lauren, lost in the spell his kiss had cast, moved more firmly between his thighs, driven by an insatiable urge to melt into him. David's breathing was ragged as he tore his mouth from hers and rained kisses on her face and neck. Lauren tilted her face up to thrill beneath the mind-stopping onslaught. In all her life, she had never been kissed so exquisitely. Their lips were a perfect fit, almost as though they'd been made for each other, she thought hazily as his mouth sought hers again. The kiss soared rapidly out of control, igniting an intense passion between them, as if they were starved for each other. Their breath came in small, frantic pants as their fingers explored the contours of each other's face.

David slowly pulled his mouth away and leaned his forehead against hers. "You're driving me crazy," he muttered, and kissed her lazily on the neck and up along her jaw. "What am I going to do with you?"

Lauren let her head fall back to offer him her throat.

"I don't know," she gasped, as he pulled her head back up and spoke raggedly against her mouth.

"Lauren...I..." He groaned and drew her lower lip into his mouth, teasing it with his tongue. "Who taught you how to kiss, woman?"

"You," she whispered against his lips. She looked up into his eyes and saw sheer masculine possessiveness burning there. A surge of excitement ran straight to the center of her soul.

"Oh! Hello, children!" Abigail nearly bumped into them as she came out of her bedroom. "Carry on. I was just going to use the facility. Don't let me interrupt." She smiled and continued on toward the bathroom.

They both stared after her, still intoxicated by their passion-induced fog. David exhaled regretfully, led her back into the living room and pulled her down next to him on the couch.

"Just as well." He looked at her ruefully. "This way I can keep my promise about no funny business." His head fell back on the couch. "Lauren, honey, you almost make me wish we were married."

Abigail toddled back into her room. "'Night, dearies," she sang out.

"'Night," they both called back. He turned and looked seriously into her eyes.

"Thank you," he said sincerely.

"For what?"

"For dinner." He smiled at the color in her cheeks. "For sharing your terrific family with me and Gran. For sharing yourself."

"It was nothing."

"It was everything." He squeezed her hand. "Tonight, for the first time in my life, I felt like part of a real family. I'll never forget it. Thank you."

"You're welcome."

"Now go home. Before I forget you're not my wife."

Chapter Seven

The phone rang the next morning while Lauren was in the shower. Dripping wet, she grabbed her towel and robe, ran to her bedroom and lunged for the nightstand. Disappointment was evident in her voice when she discovered the caller was not David.

"Oh, hi, Edna." She sighed, sinking down on the edge of her bed.

"Lauren, I know I'm probably the last person you want to hear from on your vacation, but we are really in a pickle down here," Edna said, apologizing.

Jamming the phone between her ear and shoulder, Lauren began to rub her hair dry with the towel. "What's the problem?"

"You're not going to believe this, but Ben's in traction at Seattle General Hospital. It seems he had a—" Edna paused to clear her throat "—limbo accident."

Lauren pulled the receiver away from her head and looked strangely at it. "What the heck is a limbo accident?" she asked, puzzled.

"Do you remember that series he was covering on dance trends in the Northwest? Apparently he was participating in a limbo dance contest as part of the story. The crowd started chanting, 'How low can you go?' Ben showed them. Needless to say, his back went out in the middle of his live report, and he had to bail out to a commercial break."

"That's too bad." Lauren struggled to swallow her mirth. Ben was a constant thorn in her side. "I suppose you need me to fill in for him?" she asked reluctantly.

"I'm afraid so." Edna sounded truly sorry. "Just for the Wednesday-night show. Everything else is covered. I'm finishing Ben's dance series, and Frank wants you to anchor with Rob. I feel bad about this, Lauren. We really hate to interrupt your vacation."

"It's okay. I wasn't doing anything special anyway." *If they only knew.* "I'll be in Wednesday afternoon, then, before the show."

"Thanks, Lauren. You're a lifesaver. See you Wednesday."

Lauren dropped the phone into its cradle, frowning at the dilemma she'd just created for herself. How would she get away for the evening? How would they keep Abigail from watching her favorite news show? David would think of something.

David. Vivid thoughts of last night's kiss swarmed into her head. Why hadn't anyone ever told her how wonderful a kiss could be? She'd never have believed it, anyway, she supposed. Hot currents of fire ran up and down her spine at the thought of his passion-filled eyes. It was hard to believe that only one week ago today she'd "moved in" with David.

In some ways, she felt as if she'd always known him. Always been with him. Looking around her room, she wondered what would become of their relationship once their "marriage" had dissolved. After all, this unholy state of chaos couldn't last forever, could it? She would just have to cross that bridge when she came to it. At least she knew where David stood on the marriage issue. So why did that depress her?

David was still in bed late Sunday morning. Exhausted from his fitful night sleep, he lay there and thought about Lauren. And their kiss. And kissing Lauren again. Oh, baby, what a kiss. He rolled over and groaned. What on earth was this woman doing to him?

"What are you doing? Sleeping the day away?" Lauren's head poked through his bedroom door. "You'd better get up, lazybones. Gran is in the shower already."

She looked so fresh and beautiful, standing there smiling down at him. David had to resist the incredible urge to reach out and drag her into bed with him. What harm would it do? After all, they *were* married. Sort of.

"Come on, David," Lauren coaxed. "Get up. I have something to discuss with you, before Gran comes out."

"Okay," he croaked, his need for her clouding his sleepy voice. "I'll be right there."

Lauren gently shut the bedroom door. David sat up and ran his fingers through his messy hair and across his unshaven face. "I must look like hell," he said to Hairball, who leaped into bed with him. "That's great. Just like everything else in my life at the moment. A wife who's driving me crazy because she's not really my wife, and I want her to be, but she doesn't want to be, and I don't really want her to want it, and now she probably wants to discuss this whole mess, and she looks terrific and I look like hell."

"Meah," Hairball answered.

"Oh, shut up."

How could one man look so heavenly, just waking up in the morning? Unshaven and unshowered, and still David looked good enough to eat. Lauren wandered into the living room to wait for him. She didn't have long.

"That was quick," she murmured, taking in the view of David in nothing but those damn tight blue jeans, towel-drying his damp head.

"You got my curiosity up. What gives?" His arm muscles rippled as he ran the towel back and forth over his hair. Strong arms. Arms that made a woman feel safe, protected. Arms that begged to be touched, caressed . . .

"Are you trying to build suspense?" he asked teasingly.

"Oh! Sorry. No, I got a phone call from work this morning." She shifted her eyes upward to meet his. "It seems that there is a problem at work. They need me to fill in for the Wednesday-night five-o'clock show."

"On your vacation?" His tone was incredulous. "What happened?"

"Ben, the other evening anchor, had a limbo accident," she explained.

He lifted an amused eyebrow. *"Limbo accident?"*

Lauren giggled. "You have to know Ben to understand. He's probably the most competitive know-it-all you'd ever want to meet. He was doing a report on dance trends in the Northwest and was limboing his brains out when he hurt his back."

"Isn't the limbo the one where you go under the bar?"

"Yup."

"I guess he's lucky it wasn't the day to cover breakdancing. He could have hurt more than his back." David's eyes crinkled at Lauren's hoot of laughter.

"I like that. Ben spinning on his head. It's sort of poetic."

"Hmmm . . . So, you have to fill in for this clown?"

"Unfortunately, yes. That's why I wanted to talk to you. What are we going to tell Gran? We have to make sure she doesn't watch the show."

David threw the damp towel over his shoulder and hooked his thumbs through his belt loops.

"I suppose I could call Homer and have him come down and stay with her Wednesday night. We'll tell her we're going out on a date."

"What will you do?"

"I could go with you, I guess."

Lauren looked at him in surprise. "You'd want to do that?"

"Sure, if it's okay."

"Oh, it's okay. But wouldn't you be bored?"

Far from it, he thought wryly. Any excuse to be with Lauren. A trip to the grocery store would be fun with her.

"I can catch up on some paperwork or something," he said casually. He yawned to prove just how casual he felt. Actually a trip to the TV station to watch her do the news would be very interesting. He'd love the chance to see her at work on her turf.

"Okay. We'll have to leave by one o'clock. If you have any trouble getting ahold of Homer, let me know so I can think of something else."

"Sounds good." David reached out, pulled her into his arms and kissed her soundly. Completely taken by surprise, she found herself leaning against his bare chest to support legs that had suddenly turned to mush. Dazed, she kissed him back, her pulse racing at this unexpected turn of events.

"We have company," he whispered.

"Oh, you two! It's so good to see two married people so much in love. It's so rare these days." Abigail's perky voice filtered through Lauren's dumbfounded mind.

She sprang out of his embrace, flushing guiltily at having thrown herself so wholeheartedly into the moment. David moved quickly to her side and looped his wet towel over her shoulders to keep her in place.

"Good morning, Gran." He smiled at her broadly. "You'll have to excuse Lauren. She just can't seem to leave me alone." Winking at Lauren, he said, "If you two charming ladies will excuse me, I have a phone call to make."

Realizing it had all been a show for Abigail's sake, Lauren swallowed the bitter feelings of disappointment that crowded, like a lump, into her throat. She was angry with herself, more than anything, for believing that David was simply kissing her because he wanted to. How many times did she have to remind herself that David had no real interest in a relationship other than helping his grandmother recover her strength. Last night he had obviously just been carried away by the spirit of the occasion.

Monday and Tuesday flew by in a flurry of activity. Homer agreed to come over Wednesday evening and visit with Abigail while they were gone. David went in to work both days, and on Tuesday evening he brought home a huge, noble fir Christmas tree that threatened to take over the living room.

"*Whoa, boy!*" David called through the falling boughs of greenery.

"Good heavens! How on earth did you get that monster home?" Lauren was flabbergasted at the tree's immense size.

"You should have seen me wrestle it into the elevator. Give me a hand, will you?" David grunted, forcing the tree through his front door.

Abigail hovered around them like a hummingbird. "Don't hurt yourself, David," she instructed over Lauren's shoulder. "Oh, my! Lauren, do be careful! You could get lost in there, and we'd never find you!" Her tiny, bony fingers kept a protective grip on Lauren's belt loop.

Struggling, Lauren finally managed to get her end inside amid a shower of the tree's needles. They successfully grappled the wayward flora into place, and the tree's fresh scent filled the air. They stood back to admire the small forest that had taken over the living room.

Abigail drew them both into a half embrace. "Thank you," she said, her eyes shining. "For a lovely holiday season. This tree reminds me of our first Christmas tree, after we were married. Bertie would have loved it."

Lauren shot David a questioning glance. "But he will see it tomorrow night, Gran," she said gently.

"What? Oh, yes, of course! Silly me." She shook her head. "Sometimes I'm so forgetful."

David's raised eyebrow spoke volumes to Lauren over Abigail's head. It seemed to ask, *Has she forgotten, or is she starting to remember?* The silence that followed was filled with a mixture of hope and sadness for Lauren.

Wednesday afternoon, David and Lauren left the elderly couple playing gin rummy to head for the station. When they arrived, Lauren took David on a tour of the studio and showed him around. The newsroom was bustling with activity as the entire crew prepared for that evening's first show.

Reporters sat in their cubicles, searching through videotapes for just the right sound bite or shot to best tell their story. Two anchors David recognized discussed lead-ins to a story with each other over cups of lukewarm coffee. An eager young intern ran quickly back and forth, delivering videotapes and messages, and the floor director relaxed and swapped jokes with the camera crew.

"Lauren!" A tall, nervous man came running up and grasped her hand. "Thank heavens you're here! This has been the week from *hell!*" A muscle twitched in his upper lip, causing his mustache to jump up and down.

"Hi, Frank. Sounds like another typical week. How's Ben?"

"That jerk? I could kill him! He'll be fine. How's your vacation going?" Frank glanced quickly at David and then back at Lauren again.

"It's had its moments." She smiled at David. "Frank, I'd like you to meet my neighbor, David. Frank produces our news show," she explained as the two men shook hands. "I thought I'd put him in the control room with Quint and Sally during the show."

"Good, good." Frank's mustache twitched spastically. "Lauren, your copy is on your desk. You can review it in Makeup. Also, you have someone waiting for you in the studio. See you on the set." Frank disappeared into the fray.

Situated on a mezzanine above the studio, the control room looked down on the anchor desk through a thick glass window. Thousands of buttons on an endless number of machines blinked and glowed. Lauren motioned to David to sit in one of several guest seats located behind the director's chair. She moved up to stand beside a rotund man who was laughing at something being said over his headset.

"Yeah, I heard that one. Only the way I heard it, the guy was a traveling salesman." After another loud guffaw, Lauren tapped him on the shoulder. "Just a second, Vic," he said, turning around and grinning at Lauren. He spoke into his headset again. "Wills is here. No, no, I think she was the one who told me." He pulled off his headset with a grunt. "Wills, what are you doing here? I thought you'd be roasting on a beach somewhere."

"I couldn't stay away, Quint. I was afraid I'd miss some of your tasteful jokes."

"Who are you kidding? I get all my material from you." Quint leaned back in his chair and smiled at David. "She can tell a joke that will peel paint off the wall."

"Quint! Don't be telling him lies!" she protested. "David, this overgrown kid is Quint, our director. Quint, this is my neighbor, David. David is doing research for an article he's writing on job-related stress." She grinned devilishly at David, whose eyes widened in surprise. Well, he'd play along. They were on her territory now.

"No kidding? Who do you write for?" Quint was clearly pleased to be the focus of an important article.

"Ahem." David cleared his throat and glared briefly at Lauren. "I write for... freelance. Freelance. I write during my spare time."

Lauren smiled appreciatively. "So, Quint, you be nice to David, and David, keep him out of trouble."

"That's my job." A petite blonde came into the control room and sat next to Quint. Handing him a bag of donuts, she said, "Here's your minimum daily requirement of cholesterol, Q. He's such a health nut," she commented to David.

"Hi, Sally, this is my neighbor David. David, this is Sally, our technical director."

"Nice to meet you." Sally smiled at Lauren. "So, I guess you heard about poor Ben?"

Lauren chuckled. "That's why I'm here."

"I hear he's giving the nurses absolute fits, constantly demanding special attention. He gets furious if someone recognizes him, and he gets furious if no one does." Sally turned to David. "Ben is God's gift to news," she explained seriously.

"Well, we'll just have to stumble through with the Wills tonight," Quint joked.

"I don't get no respect," Lauren complained to David. "I've got to go to Makeup. I'll come get you after the show."

Lauren picked up this evening's copy from her desk on her way to the makeup room. As she passed through the studio, she heard a familiar voice call her name. Tiny hairs stood up on the back of her neck as she slowly turned to find Joe, leaning against the anchor desk.

"Hi, Lauren." He greeted her casually and pushed off the desk to stroll toward her.

Nervously Lauren darted a quick glance up at the control booth and wondered if David was watching. What on earth was Joe doing here? She didn't want to have to explain him to David. Not yet.

"I was working on a commercial in studio B and heard you were coming in," he said in answer to her unasked question. "I thought I'd hang around and see how you were." He took a step closer and studied her face appreciatively. "You're looking good. Real good." He smiled his lazy, photogenic smile.

"Thanks. I'm fine. Never better, actually," she said, believing it, much to her surprise. "How's it going for you?" she asked, against her better judgment. Curiosity had gotten the better of her.

Her question seemed to agitate him, and a fleeting look of guilt passed over his too perfect face. "You mean Tanya and me?" He looked down at his expensive shoes and then back up into her eyes. "I don't really know. Sometimes..." He hesitated. "Sometimes she bores me, and...I wonder if I'm really over you."

Lauren swallowed, suddenly angry with him for his admission. Just when things were beginning to... well, to begin, with David, Joe had to go and throw a monkey wrench into the emotional works.

"You should have thought of that before you broke off with me," she said evenly, refusing to rise to his bait.

"I know, I know. It just scares me to think that you don't care anymore."

Lauren stared at him in shock. Care anymore? What the hell did he expect her to say? He was acting like nothing was wrong. Like they could just pick up where they'd left off and be friends. No hard feelings. Everything was suddenly clear as a bell to Lauren at that moment. She felt as if time had frozen as she stood there, looking at this man, who now seemed like a complete stranger to her. It was so obvious! Why hadn't she known before?

He had been able to let go and move on to the next woman so easily because *he* didn't care. Maybe he never had. He hadn't even fought for their relationship. For her. Not the way she instinctively knew David would. Joe was a wimp.

In that instant, when dozens of realizations flitted through her mind, she was able, for the first time, to stand back, apart from herself, and compare the two men. Joe and David. The taker and the giver.

For all the exciting glamour and fun of being in the limelight with supermodel Joe, he was not someone Lauren could count on. Build a life with. Trust. Not like David.

She peeked up at the control room window again and felt a delirious thrill wash over her. It was with great relief that she realized that she could never have felt this way about David if she truly still cared for Joe. As muddled and fleeting as her thoughts were, it was then that she knew for sure. She was falling in love with David. For the very first time in her life, Lauren Wills was falling head over heels in love. The realization came with mixed emotions. A fat lot of good it did her to fall in love with a man who had no desire to ever get married for real. On the other hand, since when had marriage been an option for her, she wondered, puzzled by this strange train of thought. She didn't want to get married, either, did she?

"Do you?" Joe fidgeted nervously, waiting for her answer.

"Joe, what matters is your relationship with Tanya." She was amazed at how easily she could say the words now. "Give her a chance. There must be something about her that attracted you, something you found interesting." Personally, Lauren found Tanya completely beige, but maybe she was perfect for Joe's ego. Joe would be the center of Tanya's life, and, whether he knew it or not, Joe needed to be the center of attention. Unlike David, who always put other people above his own needs.

"I guess," he said, impatient with her advice. "I found my sunglasses, by the way."

"Good. Have fun in Switzerland."

"I plan on it. Stay in touch." Joe leaned forward and kissed her lightly on the cheek. "Let's get together sometime soon." It was as though he hadn't heard a word she'd said.

"Sure," she responded automatically, but she had no intention of keeping that promise. With or without David, her life with Joe was over. Waving a final goodbye at Joe, she headed for the makeup room.

David sat back in his chair and stretched his long legs out in front of him. Fascinated, he observed the incredible calm that seemed to reign among the crew as they prepared for the show.

Quint leaned forward and peered through the control room window into studio A. "Who's that with Wills?" he asked Sally, who craned her neck to see where Quint was pointing.

"That's Joe. Her boyfriend."

"Yeah?" Quint leaned back. "I don't get it."

"What?" Sally asked, presetting the show's opening shots on her switcher.

"I thought they broke up."

Sally shrugged. "It looked to me like he just kissed her."

"Whatever," Quint mumbled over a mouthful of donut.

David's pulse roared in his ears. *Boyfriend?* He'd thought they'd broken up, too. Clenching his fists involuntarily, he watched the tall blond man saunter out of the studio. *His wife had a boyfriend?* Grinding his teeth, David fought the urge to leap out of his chair, chase the plastic goon outside and challenge him to a duel.

What the hell was he thinking? Lauren wasn't his wife. And if she wanted a boyfriend, she was entitled to him. Even if he did look like a mannequin, David thought jealously, disliking the pompous preppy with an intensity that shocked him. Why was he so uptight? He and Lauren had no commitment. It wasn't like he was going to marry her. And until recently he'd loved everything about being single. No one told him what to do, there was no one to nag him, no one to clean up after him, no one to listen to him, no one to hold in his arms...

"Okay, Vic, let's get a sound check on Rob's mike." Quint's seemingly bored voice droned into his headset. Down on the floor, David could see Vic signal Rob to check his mike.

"The rain in...buzz...pop...mainly on...buzzz...ain." Rob's voice crackled and popped over the monitor speaker in the control room.

Quint rolled his eyes. "Vic, that piece of crap is acting up again," he stated calmly. "We've got ten minutes till we're on. Let's remike him, and send that stupid thing to engineering." Quint stuffed another bite of his half-eaten maple donut into his mouth. "Chewing gum and baling wire," he mumbled between bites.

Vic moved swiftly to Rob, removed his faulty mike and expertly threaded a fresh one under his jacket. Suddenly Rob's voice clearly filled the control room.

"Watch the hair, Vic, old man," he snapped vainly, smoothing his perfect do back into place. Lauren slipped into her seat beside Rob, smiled absently at him and shuffled through her notes.

Quint spoke into his headset. "Vic, check Wills's mike, will you?" Vic signaled Lauren to begin speaking.

"Good evening, our top story tonight is an in-depth look at the dangers of limbo dancing in the Northwest," she joked, her low voice filling the room and causing gooseflesh to rise on the back of David's neck. She was so beautiful. The warm laughter of her co-workers floated around the tiny room. Her smile was natural and unaffected. She seemed so calm and in control. A far cry from the woman who just last weekend had tried so hard to make a simple lasagna. She was magnificent. It was crazy to think that she would give this up to be someone's wife. Sighing, David leaned forward to get a better look.

"Okay, at least something works," Quint deadpanned. "Let's check Edna on location."

Sally pushed her fader bar forward, and suddenly Edna's face filled the preview monitors.

"Hey, Edna."

Her head popped up at the sound of Quint's voice.

"Hey, Quint." She grinned at the camera.

"You set?" Quint yawned widely.

"Yep."

"Atta girl. We're on in five. So far you follow sports. Stay on your feet in case we need to bail out to you. The way things have been breaking down around here, you never know." Quint pulled an éclair out of the bag.

"Gotcha."

Edna disappeared as Sally punched up color bars.

"Okay, everyone ready? We're coming up in two minutes." Quint stuffed the last of the éclair into his mouth and licked his fingers.

Vic motioned to the sports and weather anchors and to Rob and Lauren, then turned and flashed a thumbs-up to the control booth. Lauren was still calmly reviewing her notes, as though she had all the time in the world. David was a nervous wreck. Good grief. How did these people do this day in and day out? And he thought his divorces were bad. The anticipation was killing him.

He studied Lauren's serene face in the monitor and compared it with the real one on the floor. She was one of those people who looked good on and off camera. How did she make it all look so easy? He'd had no idea what went on behind the scenes of a television broadcast, and he certainly couldn't have imagined this.

His mouth felt dry, and his stomach churned with stage fright, as if he were in front of the camera, and not safely in his little chair in the back of the control room. He had a sudden and amazing new respect for this woman. The woman who'd so unselfishly played the role of his wife, just to help his grandmother. He'd always known she was special, but now he wouldn't be a bit surprised if under her blazer there was a huge *S* on her blouse. He was suddenly shaken out of his wandering muse by Quint's calm voice.

"Okay, everybody stand by. We're coming up in five...four..." As Quint counted down, David watched Lauren and Rob sit up straight and smile at the camera. "Ready two. Fade up on two, music up, open their mikes. Stand-by one."

The music faded, and at Quint's sleepy command, Sally switched to Rob's camera.

"Good evening, everyone, I'm Rob Hastings."

Quint mumbled again, and Sally punched up Lauren's camera.

"And I'm Lauren Wills, filling in for Ben Whitehall."

She smiled easily at the camera, and David realized he'd been shaking. Exhaling slowly, he willed himself to chill out. His effort was wasted.

"Say what?" Quint asked, searching through the contents of his donut bag. "Okay, thanks." He sighed, switching the button on his headset's mike. "Vic, we got a problem with Rob's first story on the bank robbery. No. It's not done. Tell him, will you? Have Wills lead off with the political piece, and we'll do it next." He looked sourly at Sally. "What's with all the plain donuts?"

"I'm just looking after your heart," she said snippily, presetting her next shot on the switcher.

Quint snatched a note out of the eager young intern's hand and rolled his eyes in disgust. "Vic? Skip the political piece for now, too. Have her do the toxic-waste thing."

David's knuckles were white from the force with which he was gripping the armrests of his chair. Lauren finished introducing the hour's top stories, as Vic conferred frantically with her in what looked like sign language. Without missing a beat, she read Vic's umpirelike signals, shuffled her papers and introduced the story on toxic waste. At Quint's dull command, Sally switched to the recorded piece.

"We're clear. This piece is supposed to be four minutes long. Vic, have Lauren take a break after this while we figure out what's next." Quint leaned back and looked at David.

"Donut?" he offered. David shook his head and exhaled loudly.

"You okay?" Quint looked concerned.

"Fine, fine." David drew a somewhat shaky breath. "How do you stand the stress?" he asked incredulously.

"What stress?" Quint looked at him seriously. "This is nothing. You should be here on a bad day." He refocused his attention on the voice on his headset. "Okay, thanks. Vic? Vic? Hey! Vic! Yes. You. Tell Rob the political is ready, and the bank robbery is still up in the air. Okay, stand by."

The next forty-five minutes were excruciating for David, as he watched Lauren and her crew calmly field every curveball that came their way. When a story was late coming up, she and Rob would easily bat the cute-repartee ball back and forth till they received the signal from Vic that all was well and they could begin the next segment.

His worst day in court could never be more pressure than this. How did she stay so calm, day in and day out? His admiration for Lauren and the whole crew grew by leaps and bounds.

At last the show's ending theme music came up, the credits ran, and Lauren and Rob bid everyone a cheerful good-night. Quint, crumpling his empty donut bag, announced that they were all clear.

Lauren pulled her microphone off and sat back in her chair. Usually this was the time she enjoyed the most. The postshow discussions with the crew. Sometimes a group that didn't have to stay for the eleven-o'clock show would go out for coffee or pizza and shoot the breeze. There was never anything particularly interesting to do at home, anyway. But not tonight. Tonight Lauren couldn't wait to grab David and get out of there. To go home.

She waved goodbye to the rest of the crew, quickly changed back into her street clothes in the dressing room, and then headed for the control room to get David. She found him deep in conversation with Quint and Sally.

"But don't quote me on that," Quint was instructing him. "Come to think of it, there was the time when Lauren was doing that live report on that talented-and-gifted pre-school, and this little girl stood right behind her and copied everything she did. That was a howler. Right in the middle of the story, the kid announced at the top of her lungs that she had to poo-poo. You should have seen the look on Wills's face!" Quint gasped with laughter at the memory.

"Are you guys telling David all my secrets?" Lauren joined in the laughter. "Come on, let's get out of here before they tell you about the time I had to interview a goat."

"Oh, yeah, that's a good one, too!" Quint dabbed at the corners of his eyes. "David, it was a pleasure. Come see us again," he said, still chuckling.

Once they were outside the station, David glanced down at Lauren and shook his head. "I don't know how you do it." Admiration tinged his voice. "I feel so...keyed up. And I was just sitting there watching."

"Oh, you get used to it." She smiled as he held the Jeep's passenger door open for her. "Sometimes a group of us will go out after the show for a cup of coffee or something, to unwind."

David shut her door, came around and got in behind the wheel.

"Would you like to do it now?" he asked before he started the engine.

"Pardon me?" A surprised look of embarrassment quickly crossed her face.

"Go for a cup of coffee," he explained, grinning.

Lauren laughed nervously. "Oh! That would be fine."

"You know, it just occurred to me that we have never been out together." David pulled the Jeep out into traffic. "Kind of strange, considering we're practically married and all..."

"Yes, that's true," she agreed. "We seemed to have skipped all the usual preliminaries associated with being married."

"We're just going to have to do something about that."

Lauren wondered what he meant, but decided not to ask.

The small bistro David chose was crowded for a Wednesday night. A glass dessert case was filled with exotic-looking confections of every variety. Lauren scanned the menu, bewildered by the amazing possibilities.

"How on earth are you supposed to decide?" she asked.

"I recommend the Disgustingly Rich and Fattening Cheesecake."

"Okay." She grinned at the silly name. "What are you having?"

"I think I'll have the Evilly Sinful and Naughty Devil's Food Cake." He closed his menu and smiled at her. "We can try two different things that way."

Lauren glanced around the dimly lit, romantic room. Antiques were crammed into every spare nook and cranny, and live greenery seemed to sprout everywhere. The room had a warm, intimate quality, even though it was crowded to bursting with people. She looked back at David, and found him watching her.

"How did you find this place?" she queried, flushing slightly under his scrutiny.

"A client brought me here once and turned me on to the house specialty, Insanely Nuts Pecan Pie, and I was a convert."

"How do you stay in such good shape, eating like that?" she asked, and then immediately wished she hadn't. Nothing like broadcasting that she'd been studying his fabulous body. He didn't seem to notice.

"I work out. Racquetball, weights, that sort of thing. What about you? How do you stay in such great shape?" His eyes roved up and down her body teasingly.

"Same. Aerobics, mainly, but I love a good racquetball game."

"We'll have to play sometime," he suggested, and leaned back to allow the waiter to pick up their menus.

"Are you ready?" the waiter asked, looking at Lauren thoughtfully.

David looked with impatience at the spellbound waiter. "The lady will have the cheesecake, and I'll have the devil's food. And two coffees." He glared at the waiter, who was still studying Lauren.

"Have you been in here before?" he asked, and jotted down their order, his eyes never leaving her face.

"No, this is my first time." She smiled up at him.

"Do I know you?" The waiter grinned. "I mean, do you know me?"

"I don't think so. Maybe I look like someone you know?"

"Hmmm... No. I'll think of it." Completely ignoring David, he wandered off, still deep in thought. David bristled.

"He recognized you."

"Yes."

"Doesn't that bother you?"

"It's part of the deal. It happens all the time." She shrugged.

"It would drive me crazy," he said huffily.

"You'd get used to it." Her mouth lifted in amusement at his impatience with her admiring public. He seemed almost jealous. *No,* she thought, *stop being ridiculous.* Wishing won't make it so.

"So, tell me," he said offhandedly. "Why haven't you ever fallen in love with a member of your adoring public and gotten married?" He studied her with hooded eyes.

"Just never met the right guy, I guess. In my field, if you're ambitious, there isn't much time for a social life." She plucked nervously at her napkin.

"I can't believe you've never come close," he challenged curiously. Wondering if she would bring up the guy who had visited her in the studio.

She debated for a second whether or not to mention Joe.

"I recently broke up with my boyfriend, Joe. I wouldn't call my relationship with him an engagement or anything." David was flooded with relief. He could have sworn the heavens opened and the angels sang the "Hallelujah Chorus." But why? What was it to him? "We had a sort of... casual understanding. Nothing serious, but I counted on him." Her mouth twisted down bitterly.

"He hurt you." David's statement was at once gentle and angry.

Lauren's smile was self-deprecating. "Yes, kind of. It just stung for a while. My pride, more than anything. He's all right."

It was clear to David that Lauren's ex was obviously an idiot. Anyone who would throw away a relationship with her was nuts.

"How did you meet him, being so busy and all?"

"I was doing a fashion segment several years ago, and Joe was one of the models. He's pretty popular locally. You've probably seen him."

"What's his last name?"

"King."

David's eyes widened in surprise before he hooted with glee. "Joe King?" His laughter rang out loudly. "That's a riot! Joking! Ha! You must be joking!" His pun made him laugh even harder.

"Nope." She joined in the mirth. "And the poor guy has a brother named Lee. Honest." Lauren loved the way his laugh was so spontaneous and contagious. She'd never met anyone with such an infectious, delightful laugh. "What about you?" she asked when he had regained his composure.

"What about me what?"

"Why hasn't a bright up-and-coming lawyer like you ever made a trip to the altar?"

He pondered her question thoughtfully. "Just never met the right woman, I guess. In my field, if you're smart, you learn from everyone else's mistakes. I realized at an early age that you can't trust the institution." His expression was sardonic.

"You've seen a lot of hurt," she said simply, bringing their conversation full circle.

"Yes. But don't get me wrong. I have nothing against marriage—for other people. Fighting over alimony and child support just isn't my idea of a day in the park."

"It doesn't have to be that way." Lauren could have bitten her tongue off. *Now he probably thinks I want to get married,* she thought, annoyed with her big mouth.

"I know. Gran and Grandpa Bertie were a good example. But those were the good old days. And then, of course, there is us." His eyes twinkled at her.

"Of course," she said, teasing him back. "By today's standards, we're old marrieds."

David's expression grew warm. "You were really great tonight. I had no idea what it took to do your job. I'm really impressed."

Much to David's dismay, the waiter chose that moment to return with their coffee and desserts.

"Lauren Wills, evening news," he announced proudly, as though she might be unaware of her identity.

"Right." Lauren smiled patiently.

"I *love* your show! Can I have your autograph?" he asked, eagerly shoving his menu book and pen into her hands.

"Sure, what's your name?"

"Ralph."

"Okay, Ralph, here you go." She scribbled him a quick message and handed his pad and pen back.

"Thank you, Ms. Wills." He glanced at David. "You, too, Mr. Wills." With a happy grin, he disappeared into the kitchen.

Lauren was afraid to look at David. He must be furious, and she wouldn't blame him. The waiter's assumption was natural, and it wasn't the first time it had happened to her when she was out with a man. But this was different. This was David. He was not some Caspar Milquetoast, happy to live in her shadow, to be the wind beneath her wings. Oh, no. David was his own man. Strong, independent and... What was that? Casting a nervous glance in his direction, she heard it again. He was chuckling.

"What's so funny?" She smiled tentatively.

"Mr. Wills. I like that. No one has ever called me that before."

"Probably because it's not your name." Her smile broadened. "I take it that doesn't bother you?"

"No. Why should it?"

She lifted her shoulders lightly. "It always bothered Joe."

"Joe was an egomaniac."

"Yes. He was." Lauren suddenly felt inexplicably happy.

Chapter Eight

Friday, the twenty-second of December, arrived on a brilliant, cloudless day. It seemed as if everyone in the entire Seattle area had decided to take advantage of the break in the bad weather and head downtown to shop. Lauren searched the faces of the milling throng for a glimpse of Polly. Heaven only knew what was keeping her so long, Lauren fumed to herself. She'd probably glued herself to one of her infamous craft projects and couldn't get out of her house. It had been Polly's idea to go dress shopping in the first place. Lauren had been content to make do with something in her closet, but Polly had insisted.

Lauren sighed and walked back inside the department store. Maybe she'd missed her coming in through another door. People passing by smiled and nudged one another, recognizing their local news anchor. Being used to the stares and smiles of strangers, Lauren didn't even notice.

Pressure shopping, that was what this was. If David thought her job was stressful, he should try shopping for the perfect dress just hours before the mayor's Christmas ball.

Where was she, anyway? Lauren checked her watch for the umpteenth time.

"Have you been waiting long?" Breathless and pink-cheeked, Polly ran up to Lauren, nearly colliding with a little boy in the process. "Sorry, sweetie." Polly smiled and patted his towhead.

"Don't 'Sorry sweetie' me! Where have you been?" Lauren groused, checking her watch yet again. "Do you realize we only have about two hours to try on dozens of dresses, change our minds, dodge pushy salesclerks, change our minds, go to a different store, change our minds, and ultimately spend a fortune on a dress that isn't really what we want?"

"Don't you just love it?" Polly beamed.

"No."

The next two hours were spent doing exactly what Lauren had been afraid of. Polly would herd her into a dressing room and toss dresses on the top of the stall and then wait for Lauren to come out and model for her.

"Oh! Yes! That's you!" Polly was loudly impressed with each dress Lauren tried on.

"Yes, it's me, if I'm going to a square dance." Lauren flounced back into the dressing room to change.

"Oh, yes! I love it!" Polly gushed over the next ensemble.

"Polly, I swear, you're trying to get me on Mr. Blackwell's worst-dressed list. Isn't there anything with a few less bows? And what's with this bird?" Lauren gestured to the winged apparition perched on her shoulder.

"I see your point. Why are you so tense? You're certainly not worried about impressing David, are you?" Polly called into the dressing room.

"I don't know. Ouch!" Lauren's muffled voice came back. "I guess it's a little of that, and...well...Joe and Tanya will be there, and you know how I feel about that...."

"Not really." Polly frowned. "How *do* you feel about that?"

"Awkward! I truly don't have any desire to spend another minute in Joe's company. It irritates me that he thinks
we can still be friends."

"Sounds like David has helped heal your boo-boo feelings."

Lauren giggled. "Oh, yes, he's helped more than he
knows— Ouch! This bird keeps pecking me!"

"He's mad at you. So, tell me, how's the wife business
going? Is being married the horror you thought it would
be?"

Lauren grunted, groaned, and finally tossed the bird dress
over the stall at Polly. "You know what's scary? Its not
horrible at all. In fact, it's probably the most fun I've ever
had in my life."

"Really?" Polly stared at the stall door in shock.

"I don't know why, but yes. I could never see what the big
attraction was for, you know, staying home and being a wife
and a mom, but now...I'm beginning to understand."
Lauren emerged from the dressing room in a flowing organza concoction with large, winglike sleeves. "I feel like
Scarlett O'Hara in this get-up, Pol. I'm not going to the
prom here," she complained.

Polly eyed her friend critically. "Okay, okay. Hmmm...
All that's left is this little black thing."

"Give it here. Let's get this show on the road," she
mumbled, struggling with the organza.

"I wonder what Tanya will be wearing?" Polly mused
aloud.

"Who knows? She and Joe are probably going to wear
matching whips and chains, or something equally disgusting. Hey! We may be on to something here."

Lauren could tell by the way Polly's mouth dropped open
that they had finally found *the* dress. The black satin dress
that had hung so unappealingly on the hanger clung to her
figure like a second skin. The deep black satin accented the
creamy softness of her complexion and matched the highlights in her hair. It was cut low in the front and high on the
thigh, and Lauren couldn't help but feel somewhat naked.

"Wow. That's it. *That is it!* I mean it! Look no further," Polly enthused. "Go home and get dressed, girl!"

Later that evening, as Lauren put the final touches on her makeup and stood back to survey herself in the mirror, she began to wonder if maybe the dress wasn't a bit much. Nervously she nibbled her lower lip and wondered if she had time to change into something more conservative. Low-cut and sexy wasn't really her style, but she had to admit that the dress made her feel daring. But maybe Polly'd been wrong. After all, she'd liked the organza.

A soft knock came at David's bedroom door, and his voice called, "Lauren, are you decent?"

"That depends," she answered uncertainly.

The door opened a crack, and David peeked in. "Homer will be here . . . soon." He whistled softly as he pushed the door open and came inside the bedroom. "Wow, you look terrific." His eyes were wide with appreciation.

She looked up at him and smiled. "You look pretty wonderful yourself," she told him, taking in his crisp black tuxedo and his black satin cummerbund. His bow tie was hanging untied around his neck, and his collar was unbuttoned. Her heart pounded erratically beneath her breast. He looked so incredibly sexy, she could hardly breathe.

The jacket accentuated the width of his broad shoulders, and his pants fitted snugly, but not too tightly, across his thighs. His left cheek dimpled engagingly as he took in her appearance.

"I love the dress," he said admiringly, and Lauren was instantly filled with relief. "But mostly I love the way you fill it."

"You don't think it's too . . . risqué?" she asked shyly.

"I think it's perfect."

His eyes stabbed into hers, and, though they didn't say anything, their look spoke volumes. David cleared his throat and shook his head slightly, as though trying to resurface from a dream. It was getting increasingly difficult to re-

main emotionally detached from this woman. She never
stopped surprising him.

Everything about her excited him wildly, and, much to his
surprise, he found he was beginning to think of them as a
couple. It was with a certain amount of discomfort that he
realized he was really going to miss living with her when
Gran got well and things went back to normal. Miss her,
nothing. Hell, he'd be a mess, and he knew it. Somehow,
living across the hall from her just wouldn't be the same. He
shoved the niggling sadness to the back of his mind and
grinned at her.

"Could you give me a hand with this?" He gestured toward his tie.

"I can try." She stepped forward and reached up to button his collar. The feminine scent that was uniquely Lauren
filled his senses, threatening to intoxicate him. Her breath
lightly tickled his chin as she concentrated on his tie.

"I used to have to do this for Zach and my Dad once in a
while. There's a trick to it." Her fingers deftly knotted the
bow.

"Zach in a bow tie? That's interesting."

"No, that's a miracle. My mother can be a bit of a drill
sergeant when the occasion calls for it. Never underesti-
mate the power of a woman." Finishing, she looked up into
his eyes, their faces mere inches apart.

"I don't," he said, his lips hovering lightly over hers as he
spoke, almost, but not quite, touching them.

Lauren swallowed and ran the tip of her tongue lightly
across her lips. David's eyes moved down to her mouth, and
she could feel the heat of his look as though he had kissed
her. The tension between the two of them was approaching
the point of being unbearable.

"I wish we could skip this thing and stay home tonight,
and...you know." Frustration was evident in David's voice.

"I know. Me too," Lauren whispered shakily against his
mouth. Her voice sounded breathy and foreign to her ears.

"We'd probably better go... before... you know."

For what seemed an eternity, neither of them moved.

"I know," Lauren rasped, her body trembled with electricity.

Breathing deeply, David stepped back and touched Lauren's lower lip with his thumb. "Sometimes, I wish we really were . . . Well, you know."

"Yes. I know." Lauren blushed and reluctantly followed David out of his bedroom.

Abigail was just coming out of the guest bedroom to answer the persistently ringing doorbell when Lauren collided with David's back. He stopped to stare in shock at his formally dressed grandmother.

She pursed her ruby-red lips together in dismay as she read the surprised expressions on their two young faces.

"Oh, dear." She sighed petulantly. "I had so wanted to surprise you, and now, well, you caught me." The bell sounded again. Abigail pulled open the front door to reveal a red-faced Homer, holding a wilting bouquet and looking resplendent in an ancient tuxedo.

"Bertie! My dear, you look marvelous!" Abigail reached out and pulled the reticent Homer into the living room. Homer looked as if he wished the floor would open up and swallow him alive.

"Hello, Abigail." He pecked her lightly on the cheek and turned to the two behind him. "David. Lauren." His eyes silently pleaded with them for understanding.

"Surprise!" Abigail cried, beaming at her grandson. "We are going to the mayor's Christmas ball with you!"

David and Lauren exchanged flabbergasted glances. A nameless fear suddenly gripped Lauren, causing her to reach out and tightly grasp David's arm for support. Now what were they going to do? This was too much. This was definitely, far and away, too much. So far living this sham had been manageable, but there was no way they could ever get away with it now. Not in front of the general public. Fighting feelings of light-headedness and nausea, Lauren looked up at David for help. There she found only a reflection of her own panic.

"I, uh...think I'd like to sit down," she mumbled, smiling sickly. David guided her over to the couch.

"I think I'll join you."

"Yes! That's nice. Sit, sit. Let's all sit." Abigail motioned to Homer, and they sat together on the love seat. "Isn't this exciting? Just like a double date. Are you surprised?" She looked at David expectantly.

"You could say that." David seemed to have finally found his voice.

"Oh, good. I made Bertie keep it a secret. No offense, David, but I'm feeling so much better, and I thought if I didn't get out of here and do something fun, why, I just might lose my mind."

"We wouldn't want that to happen," Homer put in dryly.

Abigail giggled girlishly. "And this seemed like the perfect thing. A charity ball for the heart fund. What better thing for me to contribute to?"

"I can't think of a thing," Lauren commented weakly. David patted her knee with empathy. He had to stop this crazy idea of Abigail's, and fast. Why hadn't Homer said anything?

"Ho—uh, Grandpa—why don't you come with me to the kitchen and help me fix the ladies a cocktail?" David stood and jerked his head several times in the direction of the kitchen.

Homer, looking absolutely miserable, agreed quickly. "Capital idea," he grunted, and practically ran to the kitchen ahead of David.

"What in heaven's name are you thinking, sir?" David demanded once the two men were behind closed doors. "Pardon me—and maybe I'm overreacting here—but isn't this idea of hers kind of dangerous? What if someone blows the whistle on our little charade? Couldn't it kill her? Isn't that why we're all going through this whole idiotic scheme in the first place?" Exasperated, David raked his hands through his neatly combed and moussed hair, effectively destroying it.

Homer shrugged helplessly. "It seemed like a good idea at the time...."

David was barely able to contain his agitation. "Good idea? *Good* idea? What is *good* about it, for crying in the night?"

Lauren's head poked in through the kitchen door. "Uh...you might want to keep it down in here."

"Where is Gran?" David asked anxiously.

"Freshening up her hair and makeup."

"Good, good. Come in here. We need to figure out what we're going to do. Homer, why don't we start by hearing what prompted this new turn of insanity?"

"I wanted to tell you for some time now, but Abigail swore me to secrecy. She can be a very persuasive woman, your grandmother." Homer fiddled with his bow tie. "She's been feeling much better lately, as she told you, and wanted to prove it by going out for some fun. And—" Homer took a deep breath "—she thought the mayor's Christmas ball sounded like fun. With you and Lauren there, she felt she could show you how well she is doing by dancing and socializing. I know it sounds strange, but she insisted. And you know what her doctor says. Give her what she wants."

"Who is this quack? I'm going to give him a piece of my mind. I've had just about enough of this give-her-what-she-wants approach to medicine," David ranted, tearing at his hair with frenzied hands.

"Not now, David. Let's try to concentrate on how we're going to deal with this problem. Homer, is it too late for you to develop a terrible headache or something?" Lauren looked at Homer with hope.

Homer shook his head remorsefully. "I've already thought of that, and I just can't bring myself to do it. She has looked forward to this for so long."

David snorted noisily in disgust. "Okay, okay, so she's going. Homer, in your professional opinion, is she up to it?"

"Quite honestly? I'm afraid so. Her doctor is very pleased with her progress. In fact, he gave her the go-ahead on this

He thinks it might even be good for her, help her with her memory and so forth.''

David looked doubtful, so Homer forged on. "She cannot stay out very late, of course, so I will be taking her in my car. I know it's not much, but I hoped that would at least be some consolation.''

"How late is not very late?" David asked.

A small smile crossed Homer's face. "We can probably only stay an hour or two.''

David sighed. "An hour or two in hell. Is there anything else you've neglected to tell us Homer? Does she have a hankering for some sailboarding? Mountain climbing? Or maybe she's feeling really adventurous and wants to try her hand at bungee jumping.''

"No, no. I think you're up to date on just about everything." Homer was now grinning broadly at David's outburst.

Lauren opened the kitchen door a crack, looking for signs of Abigail. "She's still in the bathroom. So, quickly, what's the game plan? Obviously, there will be a lot of people at this event who will recognize me. How will we handle that?" She looked expectantly at David and Homer.

Homer looked thoughtful. "I had a feeling that would be the case, so I have a couple of suggestions. First of all, I will try my best to keep her busy on the dance floor. I've been known to cut a rug in my day," he boasted boyishly. "Secondly, when we do run into each other, if there are other people around and the conversation gets...er...dicey, I'll try to distract her. Perhaps we could use a code word." Homer's brows knitted together to form a furry line. "How 'bout something like... 'Helen called'?"

"Who's Helen?" Abigail asked pertly, stepping in through the doorway. "And whatever are you all doing here in the kitchen? Don't you think we'd better get going? We don't want to be late, now do we?"

In a hasty preball huddle conference, David and Homer agreed to meet at the coat check, so that both couples could go into the ballroom together. On the way over to the ball,

Lauren and David tried to formulate plans of action for any
occurrence. Lauren found that the more they tried to pre-
plan for disaster, the more nervous she became.

"Now, what was plan B again? I'm supposed to faint? Or
was that plan C?"

"No, no. Plan C is the one where I spill my drink down
my shirt."

"Oh, David! That's a terrible plan." Lauren sounded
genuinely worried.

"Well, I could fall down and break my arm," David
joked.

"Why don't you just run over me with the limousine
when we get there and put me out of my misery?" Lauren
groaned.

"Okay. That'll be plan D."

David's hand rested lightly on Lauren's back as he guided
her into the main entrance of Seattle's convention center.
Searchlights cut a brilliant swath through the starry sky over
the city. Limousines pulled up and drove off in a constant
parade as Seattle's rich and famous arrived to take part in
their favorite annual charity event. The mob of paparazzi
just outside the front door nearly blinded them both with
the incessant flashes of their cameras. David wanted to
punch one or two of them out for harassing Lauren, but instead he'd smiled grimly and pulled her safely through the
crowd.

"Sorry about all that." Lauren looked apologetically up
at David once they made it to the coat check. "Naturally
they're going to be curious about who you are. They're used
to seeing me show up at these things with Joe. He loved the
attention of the camera."

David rolled his eyes heavenward. "I'm just glad Homer
and Gran are a few minutes behind us. I don't know how we
would have explained all that attention."

"No problem. We just would have gone to plan D."
Lauren looked around the lobby for Homer and Abigail.
She spotted Abigail's tiny form, clinging tenaciously to

Homer's arm. "There they are." She pointed in their direction.

Abigail's hands flew to her cheeks in delight. "Oh, my, this is so exciting!" She patted Homer's arm. "Bertie, doesn't it remind you of our prom night?" She raised her voice to be heard above the din of the crowd.

Homer shrugged helplessly. "Did we even have proms back then, Abby?"

"Of course we did," Abigail reminisced grandly. "Perhaps we didn't call them proms, exactly, but we danced—oh, how we danced. Remember?"

"I remember some things, yes." Homer tossed a wink in Lauren's direction. "We'd better get inside. I don't think I can hold her back much longer."

The mayor's Christmas ball was one of Seattle's largest fund-raising events of the year. Musical bands of every persuasion from all over the state took turns performing their greatest hits on half a dozen different bandstands. The main convention room was divided up by a series of low temporary partitions, giving the gigantic room the feel of a lot of different clubs. There was something for everyone, and when a couple got tired of doing the Texas two-step or the jitterbug, they simply moved on to the next band for a waltz, or a contemporary fast dance.

Each area was decorated to the nines, reflecting the style of the bands that played there. The Western-band area was outfitted in a country motif, complete with a mechanical bull. The big-band area was decorated in art deco, with bright neon lights outlining the bandstand. Though they were all spectacular, from the crazily flashing lights of the rock-and-roll area to the low-lit, fog-filled look of the jazz room, Lauren loved the symphony best.

The orchestra members all wore formal tuxes and gowns, and the dance floor was bigger than the rest, to allow for the large, sweeping steps of the waltz. A big glass ball spun from the ceiling, sending slivers of light whirling across the walls and floor.

Abigail was clearly as captivated by the symphony area as Lauren was. "Why, this is so wonderful, I feel as though my fairy godmother has granted me a wish."

Lauren and David looked at each other over the top of her gray bun and smiled poignantly. It was all worth it. The anxiety, the nausea, the duplicity. Just to see her so happy.

"Oh, look, Lauren." Abigail pointed excitedly through the crowd. "Isn't that your young friend Polly and her beau? Oh, yoo-hoo! Polly, dear! Over here."

Lauren gasped in horror. Polly. She'd forgotten about Polly and Gus. Too late, she realized that there was no time for her to explain about Homer and Abigail to Polly and Gus. Frantically she drew her finger across her throat to warn Polly of the impending disaster. Polly threw Lauren a puzzled look as she guided Gus toward the group. Smiling, she hugged Abigail around her shoulders.

"What a surprise to see you tonight! I didn't expect you!" She looked from Lauren to David for a silent explanation. Both of them made frenzied signals and hand motions that it was apparent she could not interpret. Shrugging, she plunged into the introductions.

"Abigail, I'd like you to meet Gus Grey. Gus, this is Abigail Barclay and...her...husband...um...Bert. Bert Barclay."

"Nice to meet you, Mrs. Barclay, Mr. Barclay." Gus's handshake was hearty.

"Gus is on a break right now. His band is playing here tonight, over in the jazz area," she explained conversationally. "And, Gus..." She paused and emphasized his name again to get his attention. "*Gus, of course you know* David and Lauren Barclay. Mr. and Mrs. Barclay are Lauren's grandparents-in-law."

"They *are?*" Gus looked at them in disbelief.

"Well, yes, I guess so, seeing that they are her husband's grandparents and all." She giggled nervously. She shot Lauren a how-am-I-doing? look.

"That's right, Gus," Lauren interjected, squeezing Gus's arm tightly. "You remember my *husband,* David."

"Husband?" Gus questioned blankly.

"Gus!" Polly giggled again. Turning to Abigail, she explained, "Gus has been out of town for a long, long time. Sometimes he forgets who his good friends are."

Abigail nodded sympathetically. "Yes, dear, I know all about that," she said with a sigh.

"But I was only gone for a week! Ouch!" Gus cried as Polly ground her high heel into the top of his foot. "What'd you do that for?"

"What? Oh, sorry. I've been stepping on his feet all evening." Polly rambled on. "I'm so rusty at this dancing business."

"But we weren't dancing," Gus whined.

"Well, why not? Isn't that what we're here for? It was nice seeing you all again," she said brightly, and promptly dragged the limping Gus out to the dance floor.

Lauren and David blew the air out of their lungs simultaneously. Their relief was short-lived however.

"Oh, no," Lauren moaned.

"What?" David looked around for the source of her dismay.

"Don't look now, but here comes trouble," she muttered under her breath.

"Who?"

"Joe. And he has Tanya with him," she whispered. "I think they've seen us."

David put his arm protectively around Lauren's shoulder and squeezed. "Don't worry. I'm here."

For some reason Lauren would never have been able to explain, she was suddenly filled with a sense of peace and well-being. The warmth of David's arm radiated through her, and she felt as if she were receiving a transfusion of strength and calm from him.

"Grandpa, *Helen called,* so why don't you take Gran out on the dance floor and show us how the pros do it?"

Homer took David's subtle cue and extended his arm to Abigail. "What about it, Abby? Shall we show the kids how it's done?"

Abigail smiled winsomely up at Homer. "I thought you'd never ask. Who *is* Helen?"

With that, Homer led his tiny partner out to the dance floor and proceeded to sweep her, albeit slowly, around the room. The orchestra was in fine form, playing music that Lauren recognized from *The Nutcracker* to perfection.

Unfortunately, Joe and Tanya were not dancing. They had just broken away from a conversation with another couple and were headed toward Lauren.

"David! Plans A to Z! Now!" Lauren hissed at David to do something. Anything. Just get her out of this uncomfortable situation.

"Lauren, honey. Would you relax? You're going to have to face him with Tanya sooner or later. Let's just get it over with." A muscle in his jaw twitched grimly. "Besides, if he says anything, *anything* that upsets you, I'll rearrange his pretty little face."

Worried, Lauren almost believed he would. "You don't have to go *that* far. A simple karate chop will do. Oh, David," she wailed. "Here they come. Oh, damn. Oh, damn. *Oh, hi, Joe!*" Lauren fixed a strained smile on her face. "Tanya."

Tanya's answering smile was vacant.

"Hi, Lauren. How's it goin'?" Joe's teeth looked incredibly white against his tan. He lifted a lazy lip at her and gave David a curious once-over.

Lauren could feel the tension begin to radiate off David by the way he stood up straighter and turned to square off against Joe. Steely eyes belied his smile, and his countenance was cool.

Joe moved closer to Lauren, throwing a look of subtle challenge in David's direction and grasped her hand.

"It's going fine, Joe. Just fine," she chirped, and nervously shook the hand that held hers so tightly.

"You're looking stunning tonight, Lauren." Joe lifted her hand to his tan lips and brushed them across her fingers. Releasing her hand, he looked at David defiantly. Seemingly unaware of the antagonism between the two men,

Tanya took on a bored expression. She tuned out of the conversation and stared blankly into space.

Turning toward David, Lauren began making introductions.

"David, I'd like you to meet Joe."

"Ah." David extended his hand to Joe. "You must be Joking."

Uncertainly Joe reached out to grasp David's hand, not sure if he'd just been insulted.

"Lauren's mentioned you before," David explained easily.

"And this is his girlfriend, Tanya McDonald." Lauren continued. Tanya, still somewhere off in La-la-land, didn't respond to the introduction.

"Charmed." David nodded in her direction.

Lauren bit the inside of her cheek.

"Joe, this is David Barclay. My, uh...roommate," she finished slowly. Let Joe put that in his pipe and smoke it. She didn't have anything to be ashamed of. Not if you didn't count lying to a sweet little old lady.

Joe's eyes narrowed in surprise. "Really? I didn't even know you were dating." He glared at David, accusation in his eyes.

"It did...happen kind of...fast." Lauren glanced at David for his reaction.

"I can only speak for myself when I say it was love at first sight." David put his arm around Lauren and moved between her and Joe.

Joe's smile was cold. "Isn't that great, Tans? Tans?" Joe's eyes searched the crowd for Tanya, who'd mysteriously wandered off. "She must have seen someone she knows. She has a lot of friends here tonight."

"I'm sure," David agreed genially. A tiny beeping noise came from the depths of his jacket.

"Honey, are you beeping?" Lauren asked.

"My pager." David reached into his pocket, and the noise stopped. "I must have had a call. If you'll excuse me for a moment, I'll be right back." The look he gave Joe held warning as he kissed Lauren possessively on the forehead and set off to look for a pay phone.

"Okay, you can cut the act." Joe winked at her. "I understand you're still hacked about Tanya, but come on, Lauren. You'd never live with someone before you were married." He shook his head in disbelief. "Where'd you pick him up? Escorts R Us?"

Lauren didn't respond to his insulting question, but instead watched as he dealt with the realization that she could live without him.

"So." Joe took a deep breath and folded his arms across his chest. "I take it this means we won't be getting together again, for old times' sake?"

"What's the point, Joe? You have Tanya, and I have David. We're happy now. Let's leave it at that," she said, as kindly as she could.

"I guess." He shrugged, defeated. "I'd better go find Tanya." His smile was wry as he moved a few steps away and then turned around. "Bye, Lauren."

Lauren watched Joe disappear into the throng, and then scanned the dance floor for Homer and Abigail. There they were, moving together to the sweeping waltz music. They were in a world of their own, Abigail with her smiling face tilted up at Homer, chattering happily at him. Homer seemed greatly amused by something she said, and he threw his head back with laughter.

She envied their relationship. In the twilight of their lives, and still there for each other. Enjoying just being together. What would she be like at Abigail's age? she wondered. Would she have someone to dance with? To laugh with? Or would she be alone with Hairball VIII? The thought was unsettling. She certainly wouldn't be the anchor of the local evening news. With David's approach, she pushed the images of her dismal future to the back of her mind.

"Everything okay?" she asked.

"Yes." He turned and waved at Polly, who was just coming out of a phone booth across the room. "Who needs

Helen? Nancy Drew over there wondered if we needed rescuing.''

"Did you tell her you had it under control."

"Mmm, hmm. How'd it go with Joe? Want me to go beat
him up?''

She chuckled. "He's off looking for *Tans.*''

"That guy is unreal. I can't believe he threw you over for
that Vulcan. What a knothead.''

Lauren howled. "That's it! You're right. I knew she reminded me of someone.''

"Yeah," David agreed. "But I really don't think she's as
exciting as Mr. Spock. Or as good-looking.''

He hugged her tightly to his chest, and she muffled her
peals of laughter in his jacket.

"We're mean!'' Holding on to his lapels, Lauren smiled
up at him.

"Who us? Nah. Just honest.'' He smoothed a wisp of her
hair, holding it loosely in his hand, and looked at her curiously. "Lauren...'' He hesitated briefly. "What did you ever
see in that guy?''

Her brows puckered together slightly as she tried to formulate an answer. Looking into his eyes, she shrugged.
"For the life of me, at this moment in time...I don't know.
Maybe...maybe I needed someone to fill the void, and he
happened to be there. It was exciting for a while, but deep
down I think I always knew it couldn't last. We're too different. I never really felt like I could just be myself with Joe.
I had to be what he wanted me to be. Sometimes it was sti-
fling.''

"Mmm...'' was David's only response.

Together, they mingled for a bit, introducing each other
to people they knew from work and other areas of their
lives. Everyone seemed to take for granted that they were
romantically involved, and neither one of them made any
attempt to correct those assumptions.

So far, Homer's and Abigail's presence had barely been
noticed. From time to time, Abigail would spot them from

the dance floor and wave gaily. She was having the time of her life.

"Care to dance?" David asked, his eyes dark with desire.

"I'd love to." Lauren slipped her hand into the crook of his muscular arm.

Once on the dance floor, Lauren lost herself in the music and the thrill of being in David's arms. She could almost imagine that she was in another place and time altogether. Something about waltzing made her feel so incredibly carefree and joyful. Or maybe it was being so close to David.

He looked down at her, and the dimple in his left cheek deepened. He was enjoying himself, too, which was unusual, because he usually avoided dancing like the plague. But tonight there was something magic in the air. Holding her, he could feel the passion growing between them, and he knew that it was time to do away with the no-funny-business clause in their relationship. His need for her was totally and completely out of control. He whirled Lauren around the floor, past Abigail and Homer, and she let the laughter bubble up from somewhere deep inside her. What was it about this woman that made him feel so alive? So in love with... life. So in love with... David felt as though he were living a dream. He must be dreaming, because this couldn't be happening. He couldn't be falling in love.

Chapter Nine

"Oh, Mom, it was...*wonderful*. Probably the best night of my life." It was late Friday night, and Lauren was sprawled across her bed, the phone tucked between her shoulder and ear. There had been a message from her mother to call, no matter how late, because Charlotte claimed that there was no way she'd be able to sleep until she heard how the evening went.

Charlotte's low voice chuckled across the line. "That's remarkable, considering your surprise guests."

"Yes, well, we did have a few exciting moments." And not just at the ball, Lauren thought, shivering at the memory of David's good-night kiss.

It was David who'd ended their embrace. "We have to stop this now," he'd ground out hoarsely. "Or I'll drag you inside and finish what we've started, in spite of my promise to be good. This is killing me."

Lauren ached for his touch, but she knew it was for the best. It was hard, knowing how well they got along as a married couple, not to give in to David's passion or to encourage it. But Lauren knew that making love with David would destroy her resolve to stay single and concentrate on her career. If she committed her body to this man, she would be lost. Giving up her career for, and committing to, a man who had no desire to ever be married was something she simply could not do. No use pretending, starting something they could never finish. She leaned against her front door to steady herself as she watched him turn and with one bittersweet smile at her, disappear into his home.

Abigail and Homer left the ball tired but happy after two hours of waltzing, just as Homer had promised. The rest of the evening floated by for Lauren in a happy haze. For one short period in time, she could let herself go and pretend she was at the ball with her Prince Charming. For a moment, she even allowed herself to wonder what she would do if David proposed to her. Would she say yes?

"Mom, we went to the cutest little restaurant on the bay. It was so romantic! Champagne, flowers, the works. He really kept up his end of the bargain."

"I'm glad it all worked out for you, honey. I suppose it could have been disastrous."

"We were just lucky, I guess. Abigail seemed to enjoy herself as much as I did."

"That's wonderful. I'm glad she's feeling so much better. Which reminds me...don't you have to go back to work this Tuesday?"

"Mmm, hmm."

"What are you going to do?" Charlotte wondered.

"Mom, I really don't have any idea."

"Do you know where you're spending Christmas Day yet? We'd love to have all of you over, but we understand if you can't."

"Let me talk it over with David, Mom, and I'll let you know. Maybe he's thought of something." *I hope so,* she thought uneasily. "I'm sure we can be together somehow."

"Okay then, sweetheart. Just remember, Christmas Day is only two days away."

Where had the time gone? She hadn't even begun to shop yet. Maybe she could sneak out tomorrow for a while. Lauren said good-night to her mother, rolled over on her back and stared up at the ceiling. What should she get David for Christmas? She wanted it to be special, but not too special. It wasn't like they were really married, or engaged . . . or dating . . . What did one get for one's counterfeit husband?

She reached over and turned off her bedside lamp. Fool's gold? she asked herself sleepily.

The next afternoon, Lauren spent three incredibly productive hours Christmas shopping at the mall, considering it was the day before Christmas eve. The lines were long, the salesclerks were cranky, but Lauren didn't care. She was still operating in her Cinderella mode. Humming softly to herself, she moved happily from store to store, collecting just the right gifts for everyone on her list. Except David. No, David was proving to be much more difficult than she'd originally thought.

She frowned, sighed, inspected, felt, tested, smelled, tried and tasted her way through dozens of ideas, trying to imagine David's face as he opened her special gift to him on Christmas morning. Nothing seemed to scream just the right mixture of caring but noncommitted.

Finally she decided on a new black shirt, to replace the one he'd ruined putting out the oven fire. She'd loved him in that shirt. He looked wonderful in black. Throwing in a couple of CDs by his favorite artists and a silly pair of Santa boxer shorts, she headed back to her place to wrap her booty.

Spicy pipe tobacco and a book for Homer, a Victorian Santa and lace handkerchiefs for Abigail, a cookbook and a craft-store gift certificate for Polly, a handknit sweater and golf balls for Dad, a blouse and earrings for Mom, a ski jacket for Zach and catnip for Hairball.

Later that evening, after Abigail had gone to bed, Lauren sat with David in front of the Christmas tree.

"That's quite a pile of presents. You've been busy." David's back was to the fire as he nudged the mountain of gifts with the toe of his boot. "What'd you get for Quint? A dozen donuts?"

"*The Joy of Health Food.*"

"Ah. Good choice." He propped himself up on his elbow and rolled on his side to face her.

"Lauren..."

"David..."

They both spoke together, and then they both laughed.

"You first," he said.

"No, you. Really."

"I was just going to say that there is *no* way I'll ever be able to thank you, or tell you how much it's meant to have you help me out with Gran the way you have." He reached over and smoothed a lock of her hair over her shoulder, then tugged it playfully. "I don't know what I'd do without you." His eyes held a curious mix of desire and sadness.

"I'll always just be across the hall, you know. I'm not planning on going anywhere soon," she murmured, fighting a wave of melancholy. Even if she saw him often, her life would still seem empty when she was no longer living with David and Gran.

David felt a glimmer of relief. "I'm glad. I... I've gotten kind of used to the married life."

Startled by his admission, she searched his face for sincerity, and found it. "Me too." She smiled shyly at him.

They grinned foolishly at each other for a moment, each realizing what had just been said, neither wanting to break the spell of the moment. The bittersweet emotions of fear and longing enveloped David as he looked at this beautiful woman who in just a few short weeks had changed his life completely.

Nothing was the same anymore. Hell, he didn't know which end was up half the time. But the one thing he knew for sure was that life without Lauren would be dull indeed. He closed his eyes and drew a deep breath.

"What were you going to say a minute ago?" he asked, shifting his body a fraction closer to hers.

Good question, Lauren thought. She could feel the heat radiating from him. It was so tempting to ignore his question and nestle into the strong circle of his arms. Just one kiss. They could talk later. But in her heart she knew the truth. They had just crossed an important line by admitting to each other that they cared. Nothing would ever be the same. And if they started kissing now, they wouldn't stop. Lauren wasn't ready. And, as yet, nothing had been said about where their relationship would lead.

"I . . . uh, was just going to remind you that I have to go back to work Tuesday morning. My last day of vacation is Monday, and I just wondered if you had any ideas about where we should go from here."

David sighed and turned to stare into the fire. For many reasons, he hadn't wanted to face this moment. Abigail's fragile health, for one. Losing Lauren's constant companionship, for another. He couldn't remember a time when he'd felt happier and more alive than these past two weeks. And now? Now they were over, with potentially disastrous results.

"Yes, I've been giving it some thought." He turned and looked searchingly into her eyes, as if trying to read what secrets their blue depths held.

"I'll get her doctor's phone number from Homer tomorrow, and ask him. He will know if she's strong enough now to handle the truth."

Lauren's eyes widened with alarm. "What if she's not? We can't take that risk."

David's heart swelled at her concern. "Honey, we can't go on like this forever. Sooner or later we're going to have to do something. I just don't know what...." He rubbed his jaw wearily. "I shouldn't have let it go this far in the first place. It hasn't been fair to you."

"Oh, David, what else could you do?" Lauren picked bits of lint off the carpet and nervously twisted them into a string.

"I don't know. Do you have any ideas?"

"No."

"We'll sleep on it tonight. Maybe tomorrow we'll know the answer."

"Maybe." She wasn't so sure.

It wasn't until Lauren was in her nightgown and ready for bed that she remembered she'd left the bag with all of her shopping receipts over at David's, near the tree. *Drat,* she fumed. It would be just like David to snoop around and discover what she'd bought him for Christmas. Chewing on her thumbnail, she made a decision and grabbed the key to his condo. Tiptoeing across the hall, she quietly let herself in his front door.

Lauren stood inside David's living room and waited for her eyes to adjust to the darkness. The only light in the room came from the dying embers in the fireplace and the small shaft of light that glowed from Abigail's open bedroom door. As she slowly and carefully made her way over to the tree, she heard Abigail's small voice speaking to someone.

She froze, afraid of being caught, and then chided herself for being silly. Of course it was all right for her to be in the living room. As far as Abigail knew, it was *her* living room. Shaking her head at her jumpy nerves, she took another step toward the tree and struck her toe on a package. Muttering an oath, she backed up and rubbed her throbbing foot.

"I think I just heard a noise in the living room, Rosie... No, no. Probably only the cat. Yes, very cute." Abigail's voice floated clearly into the silent living room.

Lauren smiled to herself. Abigail was obviously feeling much better, if she was up at all hours talking to her buddies on the phone.

"So how's the baby, Rosie?"

Down on all fours under the tree, Lauren spotted the bag she was looking for toward the back, beneath several packages. At least David hadn't found it yet, she thought, wondering how she was going to get the bag without waking David up.

"David? Oh, fine... Yes, our plan is coming right along."

Lauren's ears perked up. What plan? She stopped re-stacking the gifts and strained to hear the conversation in the next room. She knew eavesdroppers never heard anything good, but she couldn't help herself. This was about David.

"I'm trying to stay out of the way. No, she still thinks I'm as dingy as the Liberty Bell. Oh, I think our plan is work-ing beautifully. She's just perfect. You were right. I'm sure she's in love with him. You should see them together— What? Oh, yes, beautiful children."

Stunned, Lauren sat perfectly still, her mind racing, try-ing to make sense out of what she'd just heard. Was this just some prattle from an ailing woman? It sure as hell didn't sound like it. She struggled to hear the rest of the conver-sation over the pounding in her chest.

"When you get home, I'll show you the picture of her at the station that she brought for me. Such a lovely girl. Yes, she autographed it. No, she doesn't know I have it." Abi-gail chuckled. "Now, if we can just stick to the master plan, we'll have her right where we want her."

Lauren felt as though she'd been socked in the gut. The searing pain of betrayal rocked her to the core. Blindly, barely able to breathe, she scrambled across the floor to the front door and ran to the safety of her condo. Her heart was twisting with agony, and she was sure it had just shattered into a million pieces. Sobbing, she closed her front door and slid down its cold, hard surface to her floor, where she lay in a crumpled heap. Her mind was spinning, trying to un-derstand the confused bits of information she'd just re-ceived. As if she were picking through the pieces to a giant jigsaw puzzle, she tried to sort the truth from the lies.

Abigail wasn't sick. She knew Lauren worked for the sta-tion. She obviously hadn't forgotten who Rose was. David must be in on this deception. Abigail had said he had her right where he wanted her. Where was that? Flames of hu-miliation torched her cheeks. And what about Homer? Was he in cahoots on this whole charade, as well? The evidence was pretty damn damning. Had they all been lying to her? But why? What did they have to gain? David needed a wife?

Why did he have to go to all this trouble to get one? Why didn't he just get a wife the old-fashioned way and propose?

Fresh tears welled up in her eyes and spilled down her cheeks. Hadn't her mother and Polly warned her? What did she know about this man, anyway? Not nearly enough, that was crystal-clear. And to think she'd *trusted* him. Trusted all of them.

Lauren sat up and blew her nose in a tissue she found in her bathrobe pocket. None of his made any sense. There must be more to this whole thing than met the eye. What, though? Why would he use her this way? It was so humiliating. A shuddered hiccup racked Lauren's body. It was all so sad. She blew her nose and dabbed at her eyes.

Her head pounded with the lies. The tangled web of deceit that they were spinning. She wanted to throw up. No, she wanted to punch David. No. She wanted to get out of here, but where? Maybe it was time to go home for Christmas.

She slowly made her way to the bedroom phone and dialed her mother's number.

"Hi, Mom..." Lauren sniffed into the phone. "Sorry to call you so late."

"What is it, honey? Is something wrong?" Charlotte's anxious voice was a soothing balm to Lauren's wounded soul.

"Just a case of the sniffles." Her laugh sounded broken. "Um, you were wondering if I could come home for Christmas... and it's worked out so that I can now."

"That's wonderful, Lauren. When can you be here?"

"I thought I'd come over in the morning, if that's okay."

"Of course it is. What about David and Abigail?"

Lauren stopped and blew her nose noisily. "Sorry." She hiccuped and continued. "They won't be joining us. Something came up. I'll tell you everything when I see you."

"Okay, honey. We'll see you tomorrow."

After a completely sleepless night, Lauren got up before dawn and hastily threw enough belongings to get her through the next week into a suitcase and set it by the front door. She then pulled on a pair of running shoes and an old sweater.

Snapping on the light in her master bathroom, she caught her reflection in the mirror. Who was this pathetic waif staring back at her? New tears brimmed into her eyes.

"Just get out of here and you'll be okay," she told the reflection. She grabbed her purse and keys and put them with her suitcase by the front door. Then, as an afterthought, she went to the kitchen and rummaged through her junk drawer for a piece of paper and a pencil.

A solitary tear splashed on the paper as she looked at it, trying to decide what to write. What did one say to the man who broke your heart? She penciled his name in at the top of the paper. David.

Oh, David, why? She sniffed and wiped her eyes on the sleeve of her sweatshirt.

David: I don't know what kind of fool you take me for. But I've heard about scams like this before. How could you use a sweet old woman this way? You're the sick one, not her! I've gone away. Please leave me alone.

                                        Lauren

Gathering up her belongings, she went out into the hallway and locked her condo's door. She slid the note under David's door and headed home to her mother.

Looking back later, she'd never be able to remember how she made it to her parent's house. Still in shock, she staggered out of her car and half stumbled up the front steps. The porch light glowed a cheery welcome in the predawn light, and when the front door opened, Lauren tried desperately to swallow the lump that burned in her throat and smile at her mother.

"Merry Christmas, Mom," she blubbered. Her lopsided grin was weak.

Charlotte pondered her puffy, tear-streaked face. "Am I to take it that you have a case of the holiday blues?"

Lauren shook her head. "I'm fine. Just happy to see you."

"Lauren, I know that you are a capable, fully grown, up-and-coming career woman. But sometimes we all need to talk about our problems with our dear old mothers. So, if you need a shoulder to cry on, I promise not to judge."

"Oh, Mom!" she cried, stomping into the living room and flopping on the couch. "I'm such an idiot."

Charlotte sat down next to Lauren and patted her miserable daughter on the knee.

"There, there, honey, I'm sure everything will be okay."

Lauren shook her head balefully and, with as much dignity as she could muster, told her mother the whole terrible story. Charlotte made appropriate soothing noises and encouraged her to talk. She listened carefully to everything her daughter said and was thoughtful for a long while. She handed Lauren another tissue and stroked her chin absently.

"Sweetheart, I will admit that they all look pretty guilty, but maybe there is some other explanation."

"Oh, Mom. D-do you r-really think so?"

"I don't know, honey." She shook her head. "But after having met David and Abigail, I just don't think they're the type of people to become involved in this kind of thing, whatever it is. Frankly, I just can't believe it."

"N-neither can I." Lauren heaved a huge, shuddering sigh that jarred her body with aftershocks. "Mom, how can a person have the best night of their life and the worst night of their life in the same weekend?"

"Seems ironic, doesn't it?" Charlotte's smile was sympathetic.

"It's just that . . . I feel like such a fool. I was used. And involved in a bunch of lies, and I don't even know why. I just feel so dirty. And so stupid."

"You're in love with him, aren't you, honey?" Charlotte looked into Lauren's tear-stained face and smiled.

"Yes, I'm afraid so," she croaked.

"Well, honey, I trust you to be fair. Somehow, for better or worse, this thing will work out."

Chapter Ten

"You know, you really look awful." Polly surreptitiously studied her friend's swollen eyes.

"Thanks a lot." Lauren glared at Polly and blew her nose again.

"Sorry." Polly shifted her position at the end of Lauren's old twin bed to rest her back more comfortably against the footboard. "I still can't believe it. She seems like such a sweet little old lady. That's the way it usually is, though. Those cute little grannies can fool you."

"I should have listened to you...." Lauren's lower lip began to tremble again.

Polly drew another tissue out of the box and handed it to her grieving friend. She drew her brows together in confusion. "Are you *sure* you heard right? I mean, it's so bizarre..."

"Oh, Pol, I know what I heard. I may not have all the horrible details, but I do know one thing. I've been lied to." Lauren lay back on her pillow and covered her face with her soggy tissue.

"What are you going to do?" Polly asked curiously.

Lauren blew the tissue off her face and sighed in confusion. "I don't know. I've only had one night to think about it. But I will tell you one thing. Mr. David Barclay can go to hell, for all I care. I never want to see him again."

Freshly showered, shaved and dressed, David bounded out of his bathroom to look for Lauren. It was amazing how he looked forward to seeing her sweet smile each morning, and especially this morning. Christmas Eve. He hoped she'd like the after-shave he was wearing. It was new. He'd picked it up yesterday when he sneaked out to buy her Christmas present. The woman at the toiletries counter claimed that no woman could resist the stuff. He hoped so.

Sauntering casually into the kitchen, he was surprised to find it empty. Strange. Lauren was usually conjuring up some sort of culinary disaster by this time of the morning. Maybe she was with Gran.

"I haven't seen her yet today, honey," Abigail said as she lay back against the headboard of her bed. "My, don't you smell heavenly! Come here and give us a kiss."

The lady at the store was right. David grinned cockily and landed a resounding kiss on his grandmother's cheek. "Well, I'll find her and we'll have breakfast. Till then, why don't you just relax?"

An eerie quiet followed David as he went from room to room looking for Lauren. Where the heck was she? This wasn't like her.

A scrap of paper on the floor caught his eye as he opened his front door to bring in the Sunday paper. He picked it and the newspaper up and went into the living room to sit down.

The blood drained out of his face as he read the words Lauren had written there.

"I don't know what kind of fool you take me for. But I've heard about scams like this before. How could you use a sweet old woman this way?"

Was this some kind of joke? Who's a fool? What scam? What sweet old woman?

His stomach churned painfully at her last words.

"Please leave me alone."

Why? What had he done? He couldn't just let her write him off like this. Just last night, everything had been fine. Too fine. Perfect. A couple of people in love—kind of—sitting around talking about Christmas. And now this. Well, no use sitting here trying to second-guess her. He'd go straight to the source.

When there was no answer to his continued pounding on her front door, he went back to his place and dialed her number.

"Please file your story at the deadline." Beep.

The sound of her voice had a calming effect on his frayed nerves.

"Lauren, honey, it's me. What's wrong, sweetheart? Please pick up the phone. If something's bothering you, let's talk about it. We can't solve anything this way. Are you there? Lauren? Come on, honey, pick up the phone...." He listened to the silence for a moment. "Well, when you're ready to talk, I'm here. Bye."

Setting down the receiver, he leaned back on the couch and reread her note. She was obviously upset when she wrote it, her handwriting was a mess. *What kind of fool? Scams like this? Sweet old woman. You're sick, not her.* Sweet old woman. Sweet. Old. Sick. Not sick. Abigail. Abigail was the only sweet old woman he knew....

The hair on the back of David's neck began to tingle. Gran! What was she up to? What had she said to Lauren? Was she trying to convince Lauren that she wasn't sick for some reason?

He decided it was time to find out. With grim determination, he went into Abigail's room and sat down on the edge of her bed.

"Is breakfast ready, sweetheart?" Abigail smiled at him happily. "I'm so lazy this morning. I should have been up hours ago."

"No, Gran, it's not ready yet." He looked curiously at this fragile woman he loved more than anything and wondered where to begin. "Gran..."

"What, honey?"

"Last night, before I went to bed, Lauren and I were in the living room discussing Christmas, and everything was, well, fine."

"That's nice." Abigail looked at him expectantly.

"And this morning, things weren't ... fine."

"Oh, dear."

"I was hoping maybe you could shed a little light on this." David handed Abigail Lauren's note.

Abigail reached over to the nightstand for her bifocals and adjusted them on her nose. Slowly she read the note, and, as comprehension dawned, she closed her eyes and dropped the note in her lap.

"Oh, no," she murmured.

"Oh, no, what?" David's voice was etched with worry. "Gran, what is it? Are you all right?"

Abigail opened one eye and looked at him nervously. With a resigned sigh, she moaned. "Probably not."

David grasped her small hand tightly in his large, strong one. "Why don't you try to explain to me what's going on?"

She opened her eyes and fidgeted with her spectacles. "You know, I thought I heard something in the living room last night. After you'd gone to bed."

"Gran, you're not making any sense." He hoped she wasn't having another stroke.

"Then I realized Hairball was in here, under my bed, so it couldn't have been him. I should have realized then."

"Realized what?" He looked at his grandmother, trying to follow her rambling explanation. Then something clicked. Suspicion filled his mind at her words. Something was rotten in Denmark.

"Hairball? Gran, don't you mean Mr. Archibald?"

Abigail eyed her grandson warily. "No, honey. I mean Hairball."

The silence that followed was palpable. David swallowed, and plowed his hands through his hair in frustration. Striving to control his temper, he counted to ten—then to twenty.

"Gran..." he began slowly. "Do you have something you'd like to tell me?"

Abigail shifted uneasily beneath her afghan.

"No?"

"Gran." The muscles in David's jaw jumped angrily. His emerald eyes fairly snapped with electricity.

"Honey, I did it for you," she said tentatively.

"Did what?"

"Everything," Abigail moaned. "It seemed like such a good idea at first. Homer and Rosie thought so, too," she said defensively.

David looked at her in disbelief. "You're not sick?"

"No." Her voice was barely above a whisper.

"No heart attack? No stroke?"

"Well, I wouldn't exactly say that. My heart was acting up, so Rose stuck me in the hospital. I didn't think it was really necessary, but she can be such a party pooper. Anyway, now I'm fit as a fiddle. Well, an old fiddle, anyway..." she finished lamely. "Lauren must have overheard a phone conversation I had with Rosie last night. Maybe she came back for some reason, after you turned in."

David leaped off the side of the bed and began pacing the room like a captive animal. An angry captive animal.

"Why, Gran? Why the elaborate scheme? I don't get it. You scared the hell out of me! Not just me, damn it, Lauren, too." He realized he was shouting when he saw his grandmother shrink farther beneath the covers. Lowering his voice, he attempted to speak rationally. "What were you thinking?"

"I—" Abigail squeaked and cleared her throat. "I thought if you could live as a married man for a while, you would see that it's really not so terrible."

David's mouth hung open in wonder. Realizations dawned, thoughts processed and pieces fell into place with the speed and accuracy of a computer. Emotions in every color of the rainbow coursed through him. Stunned, he dropped back down to the edge of the bed, his shoulders sagging wearily. He had to admit one thing. In one respect, her plan had worked. Marriage didn't seem so terrible. And he was in love with Lauren. On the other hand, it had also failed miserably. Lauren was gone, and he wouldn't blame her if she never wanted to speak to him again.

"David?" Abigail searched his face for some sign of life.

Tiredly he rubbed his jaw and contemplated the small woman at the other end of the bed.

"You know, you are really something." He snorted and shook his head. "You really had me going. Hook, line and—" he let his head drop back "—sinker. Why Lauren? How did you decide that she was the one?" he asked the ceiling.

"You told us she was your neighbor," Abigail explained. "I knew she was single from the article about her in the paper. And, of course, we all just love her on the television."

David hooted. "You pick my wife out on a TV show? Why not Vanna White? Or Connie Chung, for crying out loud."

"Don't be silly," Abigail chided him. "They aren't your neighbors. Besides, Connie Chung is married."

"Okay fine. Lauren Wills it is. How did you know she'd fall for it?"

"We didn't. Homer bet me five dollars she wouldn't. But Rosie and I had a feeling she would. She seems so nice on TV, and she's involved with the Benedictine Center for the Aging. It's her favorite charity, so we knew she cared about old people."

David was nonplussed. "I don't believe this! You come up with the most...*harebrained* idea I've ever heard of in my life, and you actually make it work. Incredible."

"Well, Homer helped," Abigail pointed out modestly.

"Yes. Let's talk about good old Homer, shall we? What kind of a doctor would go along with such a debacle? Doesn't this violate some kind of Hippocratic oath?"

"I'm not sure, being that he's a psychologist."

"*That figures.* Okay. One last question. Why did you two follow us to the mayor's Christmas ball?"

"We decided it was time you admitted your relationship to the public. With us there, you couldn't go around telling everyone you were just friends. You two were brilliant with Polly's boyfriend, by the way. I thought old Homer would split a gut."

"Thanks, Gran. Thanks a heap."

Christmas Day was one incredibly long test of endurance, and by Tuesday morning Lauren was too listless to open her eyes. It seemed that there was nothing her family could do or say to relieve her pain. In the twenty-nine years she had spent on this planet, she'd never been as miserable as she was now. Never had she experienced such raw grief and despair before. For the first time in her life, all the sad songs on the radio made sense. She finally understood why people warned each other not to get hurt in a relationship.

The hurt was so acute, she could barely function. She couldn't begin to imagine how she would ever make it out of bed. She hadn't eaten or slept since Saturday night. More than anything on earth, she wanted, at this point, to curl up and die. Memories of moments with David replayed in her mind, torturing her with their vivid clarity.

The feeling of betrayal left her practically paralyzed. How had she managed to fall so deeply in love in such a short span of time? If she was honest with herself, she'd admit that she had loved David from that first handshake. Even then she had known that there was something extraordinary between them. He was perfect. Or so she had thought. How could she be so wrong about someone?

"Sweetheart?" Charlotte poked her head through the door to Lauren's room. "David called again.,... He wants you to call him."

Lauren slowly shook her head. She might as well start getting over David now. The sooner the better.

"Are you going to be all right for tonight's show?" Charlotte's face held compassion as she looked at her dejected, brokenhearted daughter. "I could call the station for you, and tell them you're not feeling well."

"Thanks, Mom," Lauren said, smiling sadly. "But there's no one available to take my place. I have to go. I'll be okay."

Charlotte joined Lauren on the edge of the bed and put a loving arm around her.

"You know, your father and I went through something like this before we were married." She pulled her daughter's head down on her shoulder and stroked her hair gently.

"You found out Dad was a con artist?"

"No, not exactly." Charlotte's low chuckle rumbled in her ear. "When we were in college, he and my best friend, Sammy Jo, got the brilliant idea to throw me a surprise birthday party. I hate those things. Still do."

Lauren snuggled closer to her mother. It felt good to be a little kid again. "Wasn't Sammy Jo the one with the huge bustline?"

"Bingo. Anyway, they plotted and planned for weeks. Everyone knew about this stupid thing but me. Then, one day, I came back from class early and overheard them talking about it in my dorm room. Only I didn't know they were talking about my birthday party. I thought they were talking about—" Charlotte's body shook with laughter.

Lauren lifted her head off her mother's shoulder and looked at her with interest.

"What, Mom?"

"Well, this is embarrassing." She laughed at the memory. "I thought they were talking about ditching me and, well, you know..."

"What were they doing?"

"Wrapping my gift. Sammy Jo kept squealing, 'We can't do this! She'll figure it out! No, No! We can't. It's too big!' And your dad kept saying, 'Nonsense, it will fit just fine, trust me. Charlotte will never know.' And Sammy Jo would say, 'Just get off!'"

Lauren began to smile. "What were they wrapping?"

"A bicycle."

They both laughed.

Quint leaned back in his chair and licked the powdered sugar off his thumb.

"Vic? Vic? You hear me? We're comin' up in five minutes. You guys all set down there? How about Wills? She ready? Geez, she looks like death warmed over. Tell her to smile or something. Yeah. Tell her the one about the guy who goes in to the bar. That's a good one." He leaned over to talk to Sally. "Sal, how long is that break at the half?"

Sally consulted the evening's commercial log. "Four minutes, Q. A couple of local commercials and a bunch of national spots."

"So, if nothing runs over, we've got four minutes. Think you can do it?" Quint turned around and grinned at David, who was sitting behind him.

"We have to." His face was etched with determination.

"We're all set up here. Got the copy loaded in the Tele-PrompTer. All she has to do is read it. It's up to you to do the rest."

David nodded.

"You gonna write an article about this?"

"Quint, old man, if I live through this, I may just write a book."

Quint grinned. "Ah. The things we do for love."

Lauren checked her makeup in the hand mirror she kept under the anchor desk. Her face looked pinched and drawn. Feeling the strain, but realizing there was nothing she could do about it, she put her mirror away, smiled bravely, and opened the show.

Abigail followed the production assistant out of the green room and down the hall to studio A. She joined David, who was already standing on the other side of the double doors, and waited for Vic to signal the four-minute break at the half.

* * *

Ben flashed a pearly-white smile at the camera as he wrapped up his segment. The light went on at the top of Lauren's camera. Quint's voice notified her of a story change through the small earphone she wore for instructions from the control room. Smiling, she set her script down and began to read the copy off the TelePrompTer.

"And coming up next...Edna Addison talks to us about divorce statistics in the Northwest. That story and more when we return."

Vic signaled the all-clear and motioned to the production assistant to bring the guests in.

Lauren shuffled through her script in confusion. "Ben, when did we get this story? I don't have any hard copy for it. Was it supposed to be yours?"

"Not this one, babe." Ben shrugged mischievously.

A violent shock at the sight of David nearly rocked Lauren out of her seat. Their eyes locked for what seemed like an eternity. She felt as if the breath had been squeezed out of her lungs by some giant hand.

"Wh-what are you doing here?" she stammered. Noticing Gran, she gasped. "And you! Why are you here?"

Abigail stepped forward and reached across the desk to touch Lauren's arm. Looking directly into her eyes, she spoke quickly. "Honey, I want you to listen to me. They say we only have four minutes."

"Three and a half," Vic put in helpfully.

Abigail motioned David up to the desk and spoke to them both. "I...we...Homer and I owe both of you kids a big apology. We lied to you both, and for that we are truly sorry." She looked at Lauren. "I'm not sick, honey. Never was seriously ill. Just a meddling old dodo with a palpitation problem. So, we came up with this scheme to force you two to get to know each other. But it backfired. And, unfortunately, you two got caught in the web we were weaving."

Every eye and every ear in the studio followed the unfolding of this scene with rapt attention. Even the control room was silent. For once in his life, Quint stopped eating.

"Lauren. That night you overheard me talking to Rosie about you being in love with David... I'm sorry I scared you. I shouldn't have been shooting off my mouth. But, I get to jabbering, and..."

David gently interrupted his grandmother. "Speaking of jabbering, I think she gets the point."

Lauren's jaw was still slack with wonder as she watched Abigail leave.

"Thirty seconds," Vic announced.

"Lauren, honey," David said. "I know you probably hate me, and I don't blame you, but I'd never forgive myself if I didn't make one thing clear. When I read your note, I thought I'd lost you. I've never felt so low in my entire life. I suddenly knew that somewhere along the line I found I couldn't live without you. Somewhere along the line..."

"Five seconds," Vic warned.

"I fell in love with you."

"Three." Vic pulled David behind him.

"Two."

Vic pointed to Lauren's camera.

Lauren felt as if everything were happening in slow motion. As though she were existing in a dream. On automatic pilot of sorts, her eyes read the copy off the TelePrompTer. Her mouth said the words.

"Tonight we're taking a look at divorce statistics. Edna Addison has the story." Lauren and Ben turned to watch the big screen TV that sat between them. Edna's smiling face appeared, and she began speaking into her microphone as the prerecorded segment started to play.

"Thanks, Lauren. Tonight we're talking about divorce statistics in the Northwest." The camera zoomed out to a two shot revealing Edna standing with a man. That man was David. Her David. Unable to control herself, Lauren gasped. Loudly.

Edna continued. "With me here this evening is one of Seattle's most highly acclaimed divorce attorneys, David Barclay. David has seen marriage at its worst and, even so, feels optimistic about the chances of a marriage surviving today. Why is that, David?"

David cleared his throat and looked at the camera. "Well, Edna, I believe that in this day and age, marriage and monogamy are beginning to make sense to a lot of people, and rightly so. Statistics are changing all the time in favor of couples getting married and staying married. Not enough to put me out of business, unfortunately, but we're headed in the right direction." He smiled at Edna and continued. "I've never been married myself, and if you'd have asked me a month ago if I'd ever consider taking that step, I'd have said no way. But recently I met a special woman who, I believe, can change all that for me."

Smiling, Edna nodded. "Do I hear wedding bells in your future, Counselor?"

"If she'll have me, yes."

"Congratulations, and there you have it. Divorce in our area—for the time being, anyway—seems to be on the decline. Lauren, back to you."

The light on the cover camera came on, and Lauren continued to read off the TelePrompTer.

"Coming up after these messages, Ben will take us to the Humane Society to meet a waterskiing squirrel. Stay tuned."

"All clear," Vic announced, and Lauren tore her mike off just in time to see David leave the studio. Ben waved her away with a few sheets of his copy. "Its okay, Wills, I can wrap it up from here."

That was all she needed. Lauren ran out of the studio to find David waiting for her, alone in the hallway. She looked at him—his face was full of tentative hope—and smiled through a mist of tears.

Encouraged, he took her hands in his and lead her around the corner and into an empty office. "Lauren, I love you." His voice was solemn with the seriousness of his confession. "I think I've been in love with you since the minute I ran into you."

Lauren's eyes spilled over with tears of relief and joy. "I have to admit, you do know how to sweep a girl off her feet." She laughed. "I love you, too," she whispered. "And yes, David Barclay, my husband, I will marry you."

David drew her into his arms and kissed her tenderly. "Gran finally got her wish," he whispered against her cheek.

"Well, almost." Lauren looked at him mischievously.

"Almost?"

"You know she won't leave us alone until David, Jr. is on the way. . ."

"True. And you know how I hate to disappoint Gran. . ."

"No, we wouldn't want to do that," she murmured, and lost herself in the magic of his kiss.

Epilogue

"Who gives this woman's hand in marriage?" The minister's gaze settled on Jack Wills.

"I do." Eyes misty, Jack handed the lovely bride over to her groom.

The last Saturday in September was warm and clear, and the garden at Abigail's house in Sea Grove was gaily festooned for the autumn wedding. Chairs were arranged around the rose-covered gazebo where the couple were taking their solemn vows. Jack stepped back to join Charlotte and Zach in the front row on the bride's side.

As the final "I do" was said, the sun peeked out from behind a majestic fir tree and streamed into the gazebo, bathing the pair in a golden light. The string quartet began to play as they embraced for the first time as man and wife.

Rose Chesterton, looking ethereal in her pink taffeta tent, wept openly, tears of joy flowing down her plump cheeks.

The plaintive cry of a tiny baby brought a smile to the bride's face.

Lauren gazed lovingly into her husband's eyes and smiled. "Your son seems to be upset about something."

"I keep telling him he's not losing a great-grandmother, but gaining a great-grandfather," David whispered, taking the baby from his wife and patting him on the back.

"They make an awfully cute couple, don't they?" she asked.

David nodded. "Yes. Now she can meddle in his life full-time. I just hope they live as happily ever after as we have since our wedding."

"I am pleased to introduce to you for the first time ever—" the minister looked out over the crowd of guests "—Dr. and Mrs. Homer Penwalt."

Homer put a proud and protective arm around Abigail's tiny waist and walked her down the aisle, through the applauding audience and into the sunset.

* * * * *